# 颐和园长廊彩画故事

## THE STORIES BEHIND THE LONG CORRIDOR
## PAINTINGS AT THE SUMMER PALACE

新世界出版社
NEW WORLD PRESS

# 长廊彩画位置示意图
# A Sketch of the Long Corridor

◁ 西 West

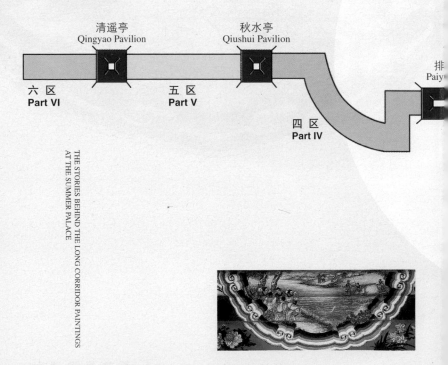

清遥亭
Qingyao Pavilion

秋水亭
Qiushui Pavilion

排
Paiy

六 区
**Part VI**

五 区
**Part V**

四 区
**Part IV**

东 East ⟹

寄澜亭
Jilan Pavilion

留佳亭
Liuzhui Pavilion

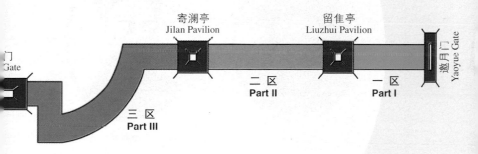

门
Gate

邀月门
Yaoyue Gate

二 区
**Part II**

一 区
**Part I**

三 区
**Part III**

颐和园长廊始建于清乾隆十五年(1750年)，1860年被英法联军烧毁，光绪年间(1886年)重建；长廊建有273间画廊，绘有8000余幅彩画，全长728米，1990年被《吉尼斯世界大全》评为当代世界上最长的画廊。

　　长廊的枋梁上绘有人物、山水、花鸟、风景彩画。其线条细腻，形象逼真，立体感强。其中约200幅人物故事彩画出自民间传说、神话故事、中国古典文学名著，内容丰富多彩，贯穿中国五千年历史，引人注目。

乾隆皇帝
Emperor Qianlong

光绪皇帝
Emperor Guangxu

　　The Summer Palace was first built in 1750, the 15th year of the reign of Emperor Qianlong of the Qing Dynasty. It was burned down by the British and French invasion forces in 1860, and was rebuilt in 1886, during the reign of Emperor Guangxu. The Long Corridor has 273 sections decorated with more than 8,000 colored paintings, with a total length of 728 meters. It was named the largest painted corridor in the world by The Guinness Book of Records in 1990.

　　The beams of the Long Corridor are painted with colored human figures, landscapes, and flowers and birds, all very delicate, vivid, and true to life. The most fascinating of them are the over 200 paintings depicting historical figures, folk tales, myths, legends, and stories from classical novels and historical records. These works are rich in content, covering the 5,000-year history of China.

## 曹操献刀

《三国演义》中的故事。中国东汉年间，公元190年，西凉刺史董卓领兵二十万抢占京城洛阳，废少帝刘辩，立刘协为献帝，自封为相国，上压天子，下欺群臣。朝中许多大臣都想除掉他，曹操就是其中一个。一天，他身藏一把宝刀前去行刺，不料被董卓发现，他急中生智，跪倒向董卓献刀。

## CAO CAO PRESENTS A SWORD

This is a story from the classical novel The Romance of the Three Kingdoms. During the Eastern Han Dynasty, in 190, Dong Zhuo led 200,000 troops to capture Luoyang, the capital city. He dethroned Liu Bian and made Liu Xie the emperor, with the title Emperor Xian, and himself the prime minister. He had the emperor and all the ministers under his thumb. A conspiracy was hatched, led by Cao Cao, who one day was discovered to be carrying a concealed sword, as he intended to assassinate Dong Zhuo. The quick-witted Cao Cao however pretended to have brought the precious sword as a present for Dong Zhuo, and thus escaped execution.

## 定三分隆中决策

《三国演义》中的故事。公元196年，诸葛亮隐居南阳，自称"卧龙先生"，有经天纬地之才。刘备欲兴汉室，三顾茅庐请诸葛亮出山。第三次终于得见。诸葛亮建议刘备北让曹操，南让孙权，先取荆州，再取西川，然后图中原。后来，诸葛亮辅助刘备，按隆中决策形成了三足鼎立的天下。

## THE DECISION MADE IN LONGZHONG

This is another story from The Romance of the Three Kingdoms. In 196, Zhuge Liang was living in seclusion in Nanyang. General Liu Bei, who wanted to restore the rule of the Han Dynasty, paid three visits to Zhuge Liang's thatched cottage to ask for his help. Liu Bei was finally received by Zhuge Liang on his third visit. Zhuge Liang suggested that Liu Bei give way to Cao Cao in the north and Sun Quan in the south and first take Jingzhou, then Xichuan, and finally the Central Plains. Later Zhuge Liang assisted Liu Bei in carrying out their plan made in Longzhong and built the Shu Kingdom, determining the triangular balance of power of the three kingdoms.

## 周敦颐爱莲

周敦颐生于北宋年间，是中国道学创始人。他为官秉公办案，不畏权贵；办案不辞劳苦，积劳成疾；后辞官归故里，在庐山莲花峰下养病。他喜爱莲花，写下了至今还在中国广泛流传的名篇《爱莲说》：莲"出淤泥而不染，濯清涟而不妖"。他赞美莲花的同时，也表达了个人的心志和为人。

## ZHOU DUNYI LOVES LOTUS FLOWERS

Zhou Dunyi, of the Northern Song Dynasty (960-1127), was the founder of a school of Taoism. As an official, he was renowned for his integrity. Resigning his post because of illness, he returned home to live in seclusion at the foot of Lotus Flower Peak on Mount Lushan. He was particularly fond of lotus flowers, and wrote a famous essay, entitled, "Love for Lotus Flowers," part of which goes: "Born in mud, lotus flowers are not sullied; washed by clear ripples, they are not coquettish." He expressed his firm will and attitude towards life by singing the praises of lotus flowers.

## 徐庶走马荐诸葛

《三国演义》中的故事。颍川徐庶为刘备军师，几番计谋大败曹军。曹操用计将徐母接到曹营，模仿徐母字迹写信给徐庶，让他速去救母命。徐庶为人至孝，见信泪如雨下，告别刘备辞行。刘备送徐庶一程又一程，依依不舍，别时泪如泉涌，久久目送徐庶远去身影。忽然，徐庶拨马而回，向刘备推荐一奇士，此人居住襄阳城外二十里的隆中，就是三国时大名鼎鼎的诸葛亮。

## XU SHU RECOMMENDS ZHUGE LIANG ON HORSEBACK

From The Romance of the Three Kingdoms. Xu Shu was Liu Bei's military advisor. Cao Cao, Liu Bei's arch-enemy, wrote a letter to Xu Shu in which he pretended to be the latter's mother, and begged Xu Shu to rescue her from Cao Cao's camp. When he left, Xu Shu recommended the master strategist Zhuge Liang to Liu Bei as his replacement.

## 风尘三侠

公元613年，隋朝危机四伏，处在风雨飘摇之中。有个叫李靖的人，心怀大志。一日，他来到大臣杨素府中，被手持红拂的歌女看中。此女投奔于他，遂结为夫妻，逃往太原。途中，他们结识一位长着满脸卷曲红胡子的人。到太原后，虬髯客请李靖夫妇到他家中，并拿出全部珠宝钱财，让李靖助李世民推翻隋炀帝，他到东南方向闯天下去了。后来，隋灭唐兴，李靖当上了唐朝宰相，东南方向数千里外也传来消息：一人拥有战舰千艘，甲兵十万，做了皇帝。李靖夫妇向东南方向洒酒祝贺。后来人称他们为"风尘三侠"。

## THE THREE TRAVEL-STAINED CHIVALRIES

In 613 the Sui Dynasty was in danger of collapsing. One day a man called Li Jing, an ambitious person, came to the house of Governor Yang Su and was loved by a singing girl with a red horsetail whisk. They then got married and ran away to Taiyuan. On the way they met a man with a red curly moustache. After arriving at Taiyuan, the man invited Li Jing and his wife to his home. He gave all his jewelry and money to Li Jing and asked him to help Li Shimin overthrow the Sui Dynasty, while he himself went southeast to make a living. Later the Sui Dynasty fell and the Tang Dynasty rose. Li Jing became prime minister of the Tang court. News was also heard from the southeast that a man possessed of thousands of ships and a hundred thousand troops had proclaimed himself emperor. Li Jing congratulated him by pouring wine on the ground to the direction of southeast. Hence, people call them "the three travel-stained chivalries".

## 三打白骨精

《西游记》中故事。唐代和尚唐僧，去西天取经。途中，由观世音菩萨代他收了孙悟空、猪八戒和沙和尚三个徒弟，保护他前往西天。路途中，一堆千年白骨修炼成精的妖怪，要吃唐僧肉，以求长生不老。白骨精第一次变成年轻美女，第二次变成八旬老太婆，第三次变成白胡子老头，都被孙悟空识破打杀。妖怪留下障眼人体死尸逃走，唐僧肉眼凡胎不识妖计，不仅念紧箍咒惩罚孙悟空，还赶走了悟空，被白骨精捉拿回洞。幸好猪八戒请回孙悟空，救出唐僧。

## THE MONKEY KING DEFEATS THE WHITE BONE DEMON THREE TIMES

This is a story from the classical novel Journey to the West. The Tang Dynasty Buddhist monk Xuanzang (618-907) made a journey to India to obtain Buddhist scriptures and bring them back to China, accompanied by the Monkey King, Pig, and Friar Sand. On the way, the White Bone Demon wanted to eat Xuanzang's flesh, believing that this would enable her to live forever. She made three attempts to do this, changing herself into a beautiful girl the first time, an old woman the second time, and an old man the third time. Each time, the Monkey King foiled her.

## 桃园三结义

《三国演义》中故事。东汉末年，公元184年，黄巾起义，威
胁汉王朝安危。朝廷四处招兵买马，引出三个人来。一个名
叫刘备，是汉景帝的玄孙，长得仪表堂堂，心怀大志，却以
编席贩履为生；一个是本地屠户张飞，生得豹头环眼，乃涿
县好汉；另一个是落难江湖的关羽，长得威风凛凛，如天神
下凡。三人相遇，谈话投机。时值桃花盛开季节，三人在桃
园中摆下酒席，祭告天地，结拜为异姓兄弟，要同心协力干
一番事业。后来刘、关、张共夺天下，青史留名，桃园结义
也成为家喻户晓的美谈。

## THE PEACH GARDEN OATH

From The Romance of the Three Kingdoms. In 184, as the peasant
rebellion shook the very foundations of the Eastern Han Dynasty,
three heroes emerged to support the dynasty. One was Liu Bei, a
descendent of the Han imperial house, who had made a living selling
straw sandals; another was Zhang Fei, a local butcher; and the third
was Guan Yu, a man of martial prowess who had become a fugitive.
The three met and feasted in a garden where the peach blossoms were
in bloom. There they swore a solemn oath to strive together as the
brothers to save the country. Later, the three founded the State of Shu.
The story of brotherhood sworn in the peach garden became well
known among the Chinese people.

## 刘玄德携民渡江

《三国演义》中的故事。刘备领兵驻扎樊城。曹操亲率大军杀来。刘备兵微将寡，自料难敌，只好弃樊城渡汉水，退往襄阳。樊城百姓扶老携幼相随。一时间，汉水两岸哭声不绝。刘备见此情景，哭道："为我一人而使百姓遭此大难，我还有什么脸面活在世上！"说罢，就要投江自尽。左右急忙抱住。众人见状，痛哭一片。刘备急令关羽催船速去渡百姓过江。直到百姓全部渡江，刘备才上马离去。刘备携民渡江一事深得民心，所到之处，受民爱戴。

## LIU BEI LEADS HIS PEOPLE ACROSS THE HAN RIVER

From The Romance of the Three Kingdoms. Hard pressed by Cao Cao, Liu Bei evacuated Fancheng City, and led its inhabitants, young and old, across the Han River to Xiangyang. Overcome by the sight of the sufferings of the refugees, Liu Bei wanted to throw himself in the river, but was restrained by his mon. Finally, he made sure that there were enough boats to ferry all the people across, and he himself was the last to cross to safety.

## 文姬谒墓

蔡文姬，东汉末年人。东汉文学家、书法家蔡邕的女儿。她自幼聪慧异常，精通音律，又擅长诗歌，但命运不济：其父得罪当朝权臣王允惨遭杀害，她出嫁后次年丧夫，匈奴入侵中原时被掳走，迫使做了12年匈奴左贤王的妻子。曹操为汉丞相时，派人带着大量金银财宝把蔡文姬赎了回来，要她整理其父的文稿。这就是流传至今的文姬归汉。图中描绘蔡文姬归来拜谒父亲坟墓，操琴吟唱《胡笳十八拍》，抒发心中的凄苦和哀思。

## WENJI PAYS HOMAGE AT HER FATHER'S GRAVE

Cai Wenji, born towards the end of the Eastern Han Dynasty (25-220), was the daughter of Cai Yong, a renowned calligrapher and writer. She was an accomplished musician and poet, but led a tragic life. Her father fell foul of a high court official, and was persecuted to death. Her husband died the year following their marriage, and Cai Wenji was carried off by the invading Huns to be a concubine of their khan. When Cao Cao was the prime minister of the Han Dynasty, he ransomed Cai Wenji, and asked her to collate her father's works. The painting shows Wenji paying homage at her father's grave after her return, and lamenting her miserable life.

## 文人三才

指宋代大文豪苏东坡、秦少游和谢端乡三位才子。传说，神宗年间，一年久旱无雨。皇帝设坛祈雨，命苏东坡作祭文，带官主斋。好友谢端乡想看皇帝，苏东坡让他披上袈裟，在坛前添香；神宗驾到，又让他奉茶。皇帝一看此人相貌清奇，便问他几句。谢端乡对答如流。神宗龙颜大喜，当即封他为了原和尚，号佛印，就在御前剃度为僧。苏东坡后悔莫及。一天，他唤来美女，约好秦少游，想灌醉佛印，使他酒后破身还俗。不料，佛印已看破红尘，不动俗念，一心向佛。

## THREE TALENTED LITERARY MEN

The "three talented literary men" were Su Dongpo, Qin Shaoyou and Xie Duanxiang of the Song Dynasty (960-984). It is said that during one year of the reign of Emperor Shenzong there was a severe drought. The emperor ordered a ceremony to be held to pray for rain, and had Su Dongpo write the incantation. Su Dongpo's friend Xie Duanxiang wanted to see the emperor in person, so Su Dongpo got him to dress as a priest and serve at the altar. The pious emperor was so impressed by Xie Duanxiang's charming appearance and eloquence that he immediately gave him a Buddhist name and inducted him into the monastic life. Su Dongpo regretted the loss of his friend, and one day he and Qin Shaoyou invited Xie Duanxiang to a feast, with the intention of making him break his vows and return to worldly pleasures. Xie, however, was adamant about rejecting secular life.

## 凤仪亭吕布戏貂蝉

《三国演义》中的故事。前面说过谋董贼曹操献刀。当时，一些朝中大臣也想除掉董卓，只是万般无奈。主要是董卓身旁的义子吕布神勇无敌。司徒王允想出一条连环美人计：先把府上美女貂蝉许配给吕布为妻，又将貂蝉送给董卓为妾；让貂蝉用情于董、吕之间。吕布趁董卓在朝，偷偷溜进相府与貂蝉在凤仪亭相会。董卓闻知，赶到凤仪亭，愤怒间向吕布掷出铁戟。父子成仇，吕布终于被王允利用，杀死了董卓。在今日的中国戏剧舞台上，仍然上演着吕布戏貂蝉的故事。

## LU BU DALLYING WITH DIAO CHAN AT FENGYI PAVILION

From The Romance of the Three Kingdoms. Wang Yun hatched a scheme to create enmity between the minister Dong Zhuo and his adopted son, a renowned warrior named Lu Bu. Wang Yun betrothed his step-daughter Diao Chan to Lu Bu, and then presented her to Dong Zhuo as a concubine. The girl had secret instructions to make the two men jealous of each other. One day, Lu Bu sneaked into Dong Zhuo's residence to meet Diao Chan at Fengyi Pavilion while Dong Zhuo was at court. Wang Yun made sure that Dong Zhuo heard about this. When the latter rushed back home and discovered Lu Bu with Diao Chan, he threw a spear at his adopted son. In the end, Lu Bu killed Dong Zhuo. The story of Lu Bu dallying with Diao Chan is still presented on the Chinese opera stage.

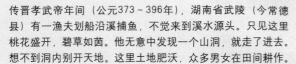

## 桃花源记

传晋孝武帝年间（公元373～396年），湖南省武陵（今常德县）有一渔夫划船沿溪捕鱼，不觉来到溪水源头。只见这里桃花盛开，碧草如茵。他无意中发现一个山洞，就走了进去。想不到洞内别开天地。这里土地肥沃，众多男女在田间耕作。

## THE LAND OF PEACH BLOSSOMS

This is based on a famous story by Tao Yuanming of the Jin Dynasty (373-396). During the reign of Emperor Xiaowu of the Jin Dynasty, a fisherman of Wuling (today's Changde County), Hunan Province, found that his boat had unexpectedly reached the source of the river in which he was fishing. In the midst of a riot of blooming peach blossoms he espied a narrow cave. Exploring the cave, he emerged into a land of bucolic plenty and tranquillity. Men and women were

田边桑树成行，屋前屋后翠竹环抱，时闻鸡鸣鸟啼，呈现一派升平景象。洞里人热情好客，渔夫一住几天。洞里人说，是祖先避秦朝战乱来到这里，不知还有汉朝、魏和晋。晋代文学家陶渊明的散文名篇《桃花源记》讲述了这段故事。

working in the fields, which were lined with mulberry trees. The neat houses were surrounded by luxuriant bamboo. The sounds of roosters crowing and birds chirping could constantly be heard. The local people were very hospitable, and told the fisherman that their ancestors had fled to this place to escape war during the Qin Dynasty (221-206 BC) and had been completely cut off from the outside world ever since. When the fisherman later tried to return to this earthly paradise, he failed in all his attempts to find it.

## 孙大圣大战哪吒三太子

　　《西游记》中的故事。孙悟空本是天生的神猴，神通广大。最初，他被骗到天上，被玉皇大帝封为"弼马温"。当他得知自己是最小的管马官时，一气之下反出南天门，回到花果山水帘洞，自封为"齐天大圣"。玉帝派托塔天王李靖和哪吒三太子带领天兵天将下界捉拿孙大圣。

## THE MONKEY KING BATTLES WITH NE ZHA

This is a story from Journey to the West. Sun Wukong, the Monkey King, was invited to live in Heaven. When he got there, he was disappointed to find that he was expected to look after the heavenly horses. He returned to his home on the Mountain of Flowers and Fruit, where he proclaimed himself the Great Sage Equaling Heaven. This greatly angered The Jade Emperor, and he sent the heavenly king Li Jing and his third son Ne Zha to capture the Monkey King. Sun

　　巨灵神逞勇出战，被大圣打得丢盔弃甲。接着，哪吒变作三头六臂上阵，大圣也变成三头六臂迎战。正打得难分难解之时，大圣使出分身法，拔根毫毛变成另一个大圣，跳到哪吒脑后，一棒将他打伤。哪吒败回天空。玉帝无奈，只好封孙猴子为"齐天大圣"。

Wukong easily defeated Li Jing, but had a harder time with Ne Zha, who grew three heads and six arms, each holding a different weapon. The Monkey King did the same, and as they were fighting fiercely, the Monkey King pulled out a hair from his head, and changed it into his own image. At the same time, his real self leapt behind Ne Zha and hit him on the head. Ne Zha then retreated to Heaven. The Jade Emperor had no alternative but to confer the title Great Sage Equaling Heaven on the Monkey King. Although Sun Wukong was no longer the Protector of the Horses, all the horses in the world are, even today, afraid of monkeys.

## 龙宫借宝

《西游记》中的故事。孙悟空修炼成一身本事，回到花果山，又到东海龙宫借兵器。龙王让虾兵搬出三千六百斤九股叉，又般出七千二百斤方天画戟。孙悟空拿在手中都嫌太轻。龙王又让孙悟空去看大禹治水时留在海中的定海针铁。孙悟空看罢，说道："太粗太长了点。"那定海针就短了几尺，细了一圈。孙悟空拿在手中一看，这棒两头是金箍，上面刻有一行字："如意金箍棒，重一万三千五百斤"。孙悟空又喊："小！小！"那金箍棒变成一根小细针。孙悟空把它放在耳中，又向龙王借了金冠、金甲、云履，高高兴兴赶回花果山去了。

## BORROWING TREASURE FROM THE DRAGON PALACE

From Journey to the West. Sun Wukong cultivated himself, and made his body immortal and indestructible. He returned to the Mountain of Flowers and Fruit, and then went to the Dragon Palace in the Eastern Sea to borrow weapons. The Dragon King ordered his shrimp soldiers to fetch a nine-pronged spear that weighed 3,600 pounds and a halberd for warding off spells that weighed 7,200 pounds. Sun Wukong said both of them were too light for him. Eventually, the Dragon King took Sun Wukong to see one of the nails that Dayu had used to fix the depths of the rivers and seas when he brought the waters under control. Sun Wukong said, "It's a bit too thick and too long." As soon as these words were out of his mouth, the nail became thinner. Sun seized it and said, "Get smaller and smaller!" The nail immediately turned into a needle. Sun Wukong put it into his ear, borrowed a golden helmet, armor and "cloud-walking" shoes from the Dragon King, and returned to the Mountain of Flowers and Fruit.

## 刘玄德江东赴会

《三国演义》中故事。刘备、孙权联合抗曹，东吴都督周瑜想先除掉刘备以绝后患。于是，约刘备过江会面。刘备执意前去，关云长愿意相随。周瑜在宴会上正想杀刘备，忽然见一员大将，赤面长髯，威风凛凛，按剑立在刘备身后。当他得知是杀颜良、诛文丑，过五关、斩六将的关云长时，吓出一身冷汗。忙上前把盏，向关云长敬酒。

## LIU BEI CROSSES THE RIVER TO ATTEND A MEETING

From The Romance of the Three Kingdoms. Zhou Yu, the commander-in-chief of the Wu Kingdom, plotted to kill Liu Bei to remove the cause of future trouble. He invited Liu Bei to a banquet. Liu Bei took along with him Guan Yunchang, a mighty warrior who had slain six generals and stormed five heavily fortified passes. Seeing that Liu Bei was accompanied by Guan Yunchang, Zhou Yu dared not move against him.

## 岳母刺字

北宋年间，中国北方金国南侵中原，朝廷无力抵抗，金兵侵占了都城汴梁（今开封），掳走皇帝钦宗、太上皇徽宗，天下大乱，义军揭竿而起。岳飞文武全才，却和母亲、妻子苦守清贫，拒绝义军重金相聘，一心报效宋朝。岳母为了儿子永远做忠臣，在他背上刺上〝精忠报国〞四个字。此时，宋康王在金陵（今南京）继位，下圣旨，命岳飞率兵抗金。岳家军大败金兵，朝中宰相秦桧私通金国，诬陷岳飞谋反，骗岳飞回京，将其害死在风波亭。岳飞虽死，但岳母刺字和岳飞抗金的故事流传至今。

## YUE FEI'S MOTHER TATTOOS HIS BACK

When the State of Jin, in north China conquered the capital of the Northern Song Dynasty (960-1127) and took Emperor Qinzong and his father Huizong prisoners, the country fell into a state of great confusion. A rebel army tried to seize power, and asked Yue Fei, a man skilled with both pen and sword, to join them. Yue Fei's mother tattooed the words "Remain loyal to and die for the country" on Yue Fei's back in order to remind him to be a loyal subject forever. When the Song Dynasty was restored, Yue Fei led an army that crushed the Jin invaders, but was executed due to the machinations of the Song prime minister, Qin Hui, who was jealous of his success. The story of Yue Fei's mother tattooing his back to ensure his loyalty became popular, and was handed down from generation to generation.

## 蓝桥捣药

中国古代神话故事。唐朝长庆年间（公元821～824年），落第秀才裴航在汉水船上巧遇一夫人，美如天仙，便写诗表示爱慕之情。那美女见裴航诗写的好，人也长得俊，便回诗一首："一领琼浆百感生，玄霜捣尽见云英；蓝桥便是神仙窟，何必崎岖上玉清。"一日，裴航路过蓝桥口渴，向一老婆婆要碗水喝，老婆婆喊道："云英，拿琼浆来。"裴航接过水来一喝，果真是琼浆玉液。再看那小姐云英，姿容绝世，便向老婆婆求亲。老婆婆要求裴航为她捣药一百天，裴航答应下来，一百天捣药不止。老婆答应了这门婚事。

迎亲那天，汉水船上那位美貌夫人也来了。她是云英的姐姐，她们都是神仙。

## POUNDING HERBAL MEDICINE IN LANQIAO

This is a legend. It is said that during the reign of Emperor Changqing (821-825), a scholar called Pei Hang, who had failed to pass the imperial examination, met a beautiful lady in a boat on the Han River. He fell in love with her at first sight, and wrote a poem to express his admiration. The lady wrote a poem in reply, the cryptic message of which was "A drink of crystal water will start everything. After the herbal medicine is pounded, Yunying will be seen in Lanqiao, abode of immortals." Pei Hang was puzzled as to the meaning of this, but one day, as he was passing through a place called Lanqiao, he asked an old woman for a cup of water. The old woman called out, "Yunying, bring some water." When Pei Hang drank what he thought was water he realized that it was really fine wine. He looked up and saw that Yunying was extremely pretty. He told the old woman that he wanted to marry the girl. The old woman asked him to pound herbal medicine for her for a hundred days. Pei Hang did so, and married Yunying. On the wedding day, the beautiful lady Pei Hang had met in the boat appeared. She was Yunying's elder sister. Both of them were immortals.

## 羲之爱鹅

王羲之（公元321～379年）是东晋大书法家，现代很多人学书法仍视他为楷模。羲之一生爱鹅。有一老妇人养一大白鹅，极善鸣，且鸣声清亮。羲之听说，派人前去花重金收买。老妇人执意不卖。羲之前去观赏，老妇人杀鹅款待羲之，羲之大为扫兴，长叹数日，惋惜不已。后羲之又得知阴山一道士养的好鹅，便急着前去。只见只只白鹅仙态翩翩，羲之求道士卖给几只。道士要求羲之为道观书写《道德经》一篇，愿以群鹅相赠。羲之书写完毕，将群鹅装入木笼，欢喜而归。

## XIZHI LOVES GEESE

Wang Xizhi was a famous calligrapher of the Eastern Jin Dynasty (321-379). He was particularly fond of geese. One day, he learned that an old woman had a big white goose with a wonderful voice, so he sent someone to offer a high price for it. The old woman firmly refused the offer. Wang Xizhi decided to go and have a look at the goose. Unexpectedly, the old woman killed the goose to treat him to dinner. Wang Xizhi was extremely disappointed. He sighed for days mourning for the loss of the goose. Later, he heard that a Taoist who lived on Mount Yinshan was raising a flock of geese, and rushed there to see them. He was pleased to see the geese dancing and singing merrily. The Taoist said that he would give him the whole flock if he would write an inscription for his monastery. After Wang Xizhi finished writing the inscription, he had the flock of geese put into a wooden cage and went happily home with them.

## 千里眼和顺风耳

《封神演义》中故事。商纣王手下有两员大将，一员叫高明，能观千里；一员叫高觉，能耳听八方。两人是棋盘山桃树成精，柳树成鬼。他们与周国作战，能听到敌方说话，看到对方行动，因此屡战屡胜。周国统帅姜子牙知道此事后，令军队舞动红旗，迷惑千里眼；又在营中敲锣打鼓，扰乱顺风耳。暗派三千人去棋盘山挖断所有桃树根和柳树根。晚上，千里眼和顺风耳领兵前来劫营，因妖根已断，妖法不灵，被姜子牙打死，姜子牙才转败为胜。

## THE THOUSAND-MILE EYE AND THE WIND-ACCOMPANYING EAR

This is a story from a collection of myths called Creation of the Gods. King Zhou of the Shang Dynasty (17th-11th centuries B.C.) had two generals, one was called Gao Ming, and could see a thousand miles, the other was called Gao Jue, and could hear sounds from all directions. When they fought against the neighboring states, they could hear what their enemies said and see what their enemies did, so they won every battle. After Jiang Ziya, the commander-in-chief of a neighboring state, learned about this, he ordered his soldiers to wave red flags to dazzle the Thousand-Mile Eye, and to beat drums to disturb the Wind-Accompanying Ear. He also secretly dispatched three thousand soldiers to dig out and chop off the roots of all peach and willow trees on Mount Qipan. In the evening, the Thousand-Mile Eye and the Wind-Accompany Ear led a raid on their enemy's camp. As their evil roots had been broken, their powers failed, and so they were killed by Jiang Ziyang.

## 山中宰相

南朝时，有一位思想家、医学家和文学家叫陶弘景（公元456～536年），精通阴阳五行、天文气象。他的《答谢中书书》，描绘山川秀美为历代写景名作。齐高帝时（公元479-483年）召他进宫伴太子和诸王读书。后来，他隐居茅山。梁武帝时（公元502-520年）他礼聘不出。但朝廷遇凶吉、祭祀、征讨等大事，都要派人进山请教于他。因此，人们称他为"山中宰相"。他一生喜欢松树，听风吹松枝沙沙作响，如听仙乐般如痴如狂。他常常独自一人去山野听那松涛之声，人们又称他为仙人。

## THE HERMIT PRIME MINISTER

During the Southern and Northern Dynasties (420-589), lived a thinker, physician and literary man called Tao Hongjing. He was well versed in the theories of the five elements (metal, wood, water, fire and earth), Yin and Yang, astronomy, and meteorology. During the reign of Emperor Gao of Qi (479-483), he was made tutor to the crown prince. Later, he retired to live a life of seclusion in the mountains. In the reign of Emperor Wu of Liang (502-520), he refused an invitation to take an official post at court. However, whenever the court needed advice on fortune telling, sacrificial ceremonies or military matters, the emperor would send someone to consult him. Therefore, people called him the "hermit prime minister." Tao Hongjing loved pine trees all his life, and liked to hear the sound of wind in their branches.

## 薛宝琴雪中折梅

《红楼梦》中的故事。薛宝钗的堂妹薛宝琴来贾府探望。时值隆冬，天降大雪，大观园内披上银装，红梅开放。贾宝玉折来一枝红梅同众姊妹即兴赋诗。分别以"红"、"梅"、"花"为韵。众人一一品赏每个人的诗句，再看宝琴的诗：

> 疏是枝条艳是花，春妆儿女竞奢华；
> 闲庭曲槛无余雪，流水空山有落霞；
> 幽梦冷随红袖笛，游仙香泛绛河槎；
> 前身定是瑶台种，无复相疑色相差。

大家认为宝琴作得最好。众人再抬头，且望白雪之中，宝琴披着凫裘，（用野鸡毛织成的斗篷，一旁丫鬟手里抱着一瓶红梅，竟像画中的仙女。原来那梅花开得正浓，宝琴余兴未尽，也去采了　枝回来。

## XUE BAOQIN PICKS PLUM BLOSSOMS IN THE SNOW

This is a story from the classical novel A Dream of Red Mansions. Xue Baoqin paid a visit to the Jia Mansion. It was winter time, and it snowed heavily one day. The plum trees were in bloom, and Jia Baoyu brought a branch of plum blossoms and asked his sisters to compose poems on the spot, taking "red", "plum" and "flower" as the rhymes. Xue Baoqin's poem was judged to be the best. She got her inspiration from a branch of plum blossoms that she had picked specially.

## 商山四皓

公元前206年，汉高祖刘邦灭秦立汉，立长子刘盈为太子，封次子如意为赵王。后来，他见次子赵王强于太子，很像他自己，就想废长立幼。太子母亲吕后心里非常着急，请教开国功臣张良。张良建议她不惜重金请"商山四皓"出山。他们是汉初最著名的学者东园公、夏黄公、绮里季、周里，隐居商山，刘邦多次邀请辅佐不出。一天刘邦与太子相聚，见四位白发老人相随太子，一问才知就里，知道人们同情太子，废长立幼会孤立赵王。后来，太子刘盈继位，就是西汉第二个皇帝孝惠帝。

## THE FOUR VENERABLE SHANGSHAN ELDERS

In 206 BC, Liu Bang overthrew the Qin Dynasty, and established the Han Dynasty. He designated his eldest son Liu Ying as crown prince and made his second son Ru Yi King of Zhao. Later, he felt that his second son was more capable than his elder son, and considered demoting the latter. Empress Lu, mother of the crown prince, was very worried and went to consult Zhang Liang, one of the founders of the state. Zhang Liang suggested that she enlist the help of the Four Venerable Shangshan Elders. These were the famous scholars Dong Yuangong, Xia Huanggong, Qi Liji and Zhou Li. They had spurned Liu Bang's offers to work for him many times, and instead lived in retirement on Mount Shangshan. The elders advised Liu Bang not to make his second son the crown prince. Years later, Liu Ying succeeded to the throne, and became Emperor Xiaohui of the Western Han Dynasty.

## 穆桂英招亲

《杨家将》中的故事。北宋年间，北方辽国屡犯中原。杨家将镇守三关。辽兵在龙谷口摆下天门阵对付宋兵。统帅杨延昭请杨五郎出山破敌。杨五郎的兵器金樵斧柄已坏，要用穆柯寨镇山之宝降龙木。杨元帅之子杨宗保帮助父亲手下大将在穆柯寨夺木，被寨主穆桂英活捉。穆桂英见杨宗保小将年轻英俊，又是忠臣之后，顿生爱慕之心，便以身相许，二人遂结百年之好。次日，穆桂英让人砍下降龙木，带领全寨人马去投宋营，才引出杨延昭辕门斩子和穆桂英大破天门阵的故事。穆桂英招亲的故事，成为美谈，流传到今天。

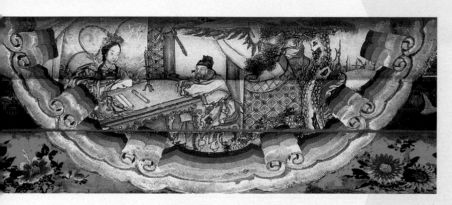

## MU GUIYING MARRIES INTO THE YANG FAMILY

　　This is a story from the classical novel Generals of the Yang Family. During the Northern Song Dynasty (960-1127) the State of Liao in the north attacked the Central Plains. The Generals of the Yang family guarded three passes. Yang Zongbao, the son of the commander of one of the passes, was searching for some magic wood with which to mend his battle axe, when he was captured by the female general Mu Guiying. Seeing Yang Zongbao's handsome looks and learning of his noble family background, Mu Guiying fell in love with him. They got married at once. The next day, Mu Guiying joined the Song forces. The story of "Mu Guiying marrying into the Yang family" has been passed down from generation to generation.

## 伯牙摔琴谢知音

春秋时，俞伯牙擅弹古琴，只是难寻知音。一年中秋之夜，他乘船夜泊汉江口。正值明月当空，秋色宜人，引起他琴兴大发，便取琴弹奏起来。岸上走来一樵夫，他叫钟子期，白天打柴赡养老父，夜晚读书，通今博古，知音律。俞伯牙每弹一曲，钟子期都能知道琴声内容。两人谈话投机，结拜为兄弟，约第二年中秋之夜相会。第二年，子期未能赴约。次日，伯牙到岸上寻访。一白发老人告诉伯牙，子期已离开人世，让人把他葬在听琴的地方，使他灵魂与伯牙相会。伯牙来到子期坟前，边弹琴边哭诉，一曲《高山流水》以谢知音，之后摔琴离去。

## BOYA BREAKS HIS ZITHER

In the Spring and Autumn Period (770 -476 BC), there was a man called Yu Boya who was a master of the zither. Sad that nobody appreciated music as he did, one mid-autumn night he played his zither on a boat on the Han River. As he played, a woodcutter came over from the bank. His name was Zhong Ziqi. He cut wood and took care of his father during the day, and read books at night. He possessed a wide knowledge of things ancient and modern, and had a good understanding of music, and rhyme and rhythm. Zhong Ziqi could tell the meaning of every piece of music Yu Boya played. The two talked very congenially and became sworn brothers. They promised to meet again at the same time and place the following year. However, when the time came there was no sign of Zhong Ziqi, so Yu Boya went ashore to look for him. An old man told Yu Boya that Zhong Ziqi had already passed away. Before he died he had asked the old man to bury him at the place where he had listened to the music played by Yu Boya, so that his soul could keep the appointment. Yu Boya mourned at Zhong Ziqi's grave, and then played his zither. When he had finished, he smashed the instrument.

## 子猷爱竹

晋朝大书法家王羲之一生爱鹅。他的三儿子王子猷做官不知官是何职，也从不尽职尽责，放浪形骸，爱竹成癖。他听说一位士大夫家栽有名贵竹子，便专程前去观赏。那家数百竿翠竹枝繁叶尖，碧绿欲滴，长势喜人。子猷站在竹前如痴如狂，旁若无人，流连忘返。天近黄昏，书僮多次催他回府，他才不得不离开。路上想着竹子可爱，又调转马头回来。此时，院门已关，子猷便透过门缝再看一遍竹子。

子猷好游，每到一处，他便命人栽竹。朋友认为临时住处不必如此费力，他手指竹说："不可一日无此君！"

## ZIYOU LOVES BAMBOO

Wang Ziyou, the third son of the eminent calligrapher Wang Xizhi, was an official who neglected his duties because he was infatuated by the beauty of bamboo. Everywhere he went he insisted that people plant it. Upon hearing that a scholar-official had a clump of rare bamboo in his garden, he paid a special visit to his home. He spent all day admiring it, until, at dusk, his servant begged him to return home. He did so reluctantly, but then hurried back for one last look at the bamboo through a chink in the now-locked gate.

## 唐僧取经

《西游记》中的故事。公元639年，唐太宗李世民派玄奘和尚唐僧去西天佛祖如来处取经。唐僧途经两界山，收了大闹天宫的孙悟空为大徒弟；过蛇盘山鹰愁涧，收了白龙为坐骑；路过福陵山云栈洞，收了八戒为二徒弟；又经八百里流沙河收了沙和尚为三徒弟。师徒四人历经14个寒暑，行程十万八千里，历过81次生死苦难，取回真经。图为唐僧师徒四人去西天取经情景。

## XUANZANG SEEKS THE SCRIPTURES

This is a story from Journey to the West. In 639 Li Shimin, Emperor Taizong of the Tang Dynasty, sent the Buddhist priest Xuanzang to India to acquire copies of the Buddhist scriptures. On his way he accepted Sun Wukong, the Monkey King, as his first disciple, got the White Dragon as his horse, received the Pig as his second disciple, and Friar Sand as his third disciple. During their 14-year journey of 54,000 km, the four escaped death 81 times. This painting shows the four on their way to the West.

## 张良进履

公元前246年，秦始皇灭六国统一中国。原韩国相国之子张良刺杀秦始皇未遂，到处流亡逃遁。一天，他途经一座桥。一位白发老人坐在桥头，见张良走来，故意把鞋蹭到桥下，让张良为他拾鞋，又让他穿鞋。张良照办后，老人让他五天后早晨来会面。五天后黎明，张良来到，老人已到。老人让他五天后再来。五天后，张良在黎明前到达桥头，还是晚老人一步。老人说，如果愿意的话，让他五天后再来。再过五天，张良半夜就在桥上等候。老人见他心诚，送他一部兵书，即《太公兵法》。张良熟读这部兵书，凭满腹韬略，帮助刘邦建立汉朝，被封为汉留侯。

## ZHANG LIANG PICKS UP SHOES FOR AN OLD MAN

In 246 BC the ruler of the State of Qin, who later became Emperor Qin Shihuang conquered the other six states and united China. Zhang Liang, the son of the prime minister of the former State of Han, having failed to assassinate Emperor Qin Shihuang, went into exile. One day as he was crossing a bridge, an old man asked him to pick up his shoes for him and help him to put them on. After Zhang Liang did what the old man asked him to do, the latter told him to meet him in the morning in five days' time. Five days later, when Zhang Liang came in the morning, the old man had already arrived. The old man asked him to come again in another five days. Another five days later, Zhang Liang also arrived a bit late, and was told to come again in another five days. Five more days passed, and Zhang Liang went to the bridge at midnight to wait for the old man. When the old man saw Zhang Liang was so sincere, he gave him a book entitled "the Military Tactics of Taigong". Zhang Liang read the book again and again, and learned all the tactics. Later, he helped Liu Bang overthrow the Qin Dynasty and set up the Han Dynasty, and was given a noble rank.

## 麻姑献寿

《神仙传》中的故事。麻姑仙子年经貌美，告诉人们，亲眼见过大海三次变成良田。沧海桑田就由此而得名，麻姑也成为长寿的象征。每年农历三月初三，是王母的寿辰。西王母娘娘要设蟠桃会宴请众仙。众仙也要在这一天为她祝寿。麻姑用绛珠河畔的灵芝酿成美酒敬献王母。因此，中国古人在为女性祝寿时，往往绘制麻姑像赠送。唐朝代宗年间，大书法家颜真卿曾在江西临川为麻姑仙子撰文立碑。

## MA GU OFFERS LONGEVITY

This is a legend. Ma Gu was a young and beautiful fairy. She told people that she had seen seas change into mulberry fields three times, and therefore was regarded as a symbol of longevity. It is said that the third day of the third month by the Chinese lunar calendar was the birthday of the Queen Mother of the West. Every year on that day, the Queen Mother of the West would invite immortals to attend a peach banquet. All the immortals came to celebrate her birthday. Ma Gu also came to the banquet and presented the Queen Mother of the West with a flagon of wine made out of magic fungus that grew by the Jiangzhu River. From then on, ancient Chinese people started to present paintings of Ma Gu to women on their birthdays. In 762, during the reign of Emperor Taizong of the Tang Dynasty, Yan Zhenqing, a famous calligrapher, put up a tablet at Linchuan in Jiangxi and wrote an inscription on it in memory of fairy Ma Gu.

## 牛郎织女

中国民间家喻户晓的神话故事。相传，天上有位美丽的织女是王母娘娘的外孙女。人间有个放牛郎，与老牛相依为伴。一天，老牛告诉牛郎："织女要来人间银河洗澡，你乘机拿到她的衣服，就能娶她为妻。"牛郎拿到了织女的衣服，与织女结为夫妻，并生下一男一女。王母娘娘得知这事，派天兵天将将织女押回天宫，牛郎借神牛之力也追上天宫，王母就把地上银河搬到天上，让他们隔河相望。每逢七月初七，喜鹊在银河上为他们搭起鹊桥，让他们夫妻相会一次。

## THE COWHERD AND THE WEAVING MAID

This is a popular Chinese fairy tale. Once upon a time, there was a beautiful weaver in Heaven, who was the granddaughter of the Queen Mother of the West. There was a kindhearted cowherd on earth, who lived with his old cow. One day, the old cow said to the Cowherd: "The Weaving Maid will come down to Earth to bathe in a stream not far from here. If you steal her clothes, you can get her to marry you." The Cowherd did exactly what the cow told him, and married the Weaving Maid. Soon the Weaver gave birth to a son and a daughter. Learning that the Weaving Maid was living in the world of mortals, the Queen Mother of the West sent a heavenly army to Earth, which took the Weaving Maid back to the Heavenly Palace. The Cowherd gave chase, with the help of his magic cow, but the Queen Mother of the West threw the Milky Way between them. However, every year, on the seventh night of the seventh month, magpies form a magpie bridge over the Milky Way for the couple to meet.

## 红孩儿计擒唐僧

唐僧取经途经号山。山中妖怪圣婴大王，乳名红孩儿，在火焰山修行了三百年，想吃唐僧肉。他用计把自己吊在树上，大喊救命。唐僧肉眼凡胎，不识妖精，只知慈悲，命徒弟解救他。猪八戒救下红孩儿。妖精一计得逞又生二计，说自己吊的时间长了，不能走路，让孙悟空来背。孙悟空背起他，他的真身起在空中，刮起一阵妖风，将唐僧掳回洞中。孙悟空追到洞口，和红孩儿狠命打斗。红孩儿抵不住孙悟空，放出三昧真火，逼孙悟空败下阵来。悟空请来观世音菩萨降服了妖怪，唐僧才得救。这是《西游记》中第四十二回故事。

## RED BOY CAPTURES XUANZANG

From Journey to the West. As Xuanzang passed Mount Hao, a demon called Red Boy hatched a scheme to eat his flesh. He suspended himself in a tree and called for help. The monk told Pig to rescue him. Red Boy then said that he was unable to walk, so Xuanzang ordered Sun Wukong, the Monkey King, to carry him on his back. When Sun Wukong picked him up, the real Red Boy left the body and floated into the sky. He seized Xuanzang, and carried him off to his cave. Finally, with help from the Bodhisattva Guanyin (the Goddess of Mercy), Sun Wukong rescued Xuanzang.

## 林冲风雪山神庙

《水浒传》中第十回故事。宋仁宗年间。太尉高俅的干儿子看上了八十万禁军教头林冲的娘子。高俅设计陷害了林冲，林冲被发配山东沧州，去看管一处草料场。时值隆冬，满天飘着鹅毛大雪，林冲到附近小酒店买酒抗寒。回来一看，他住的小草屋已被大雪压塌，来到山神庙避雪。他正吃酒，只见草料场里火起，正待开门救火，只听门外有三人说话。原来，高俅派来心腹要烧死林冲，或定他个烧大军草料场的死罪。林冲冲出庙门，接连杀死来人，迎着飞雪，投奔梁山泊去了。

## LIN CHONG STAYS AT THE TEMPLE OF THE MOUNTAIN GOD

From Outlaws of the Marsh. During the reign of Emperor Renzong (1023-1032) of the Song Dynasty. Gao Qiu's adopted son fell in love with Lin Chong's wife, and Gao Qiu got Lin Chong exiled to a remote area, where he was put in charge of a government farm. One day it snowed heavily, and Lin Chong's hut collapsed, and so he sought shelter in the Temple of the Mountain God. Looking out of the window, he saw that the farm was on fire. He heard three men talking outside the temple. They were Gao Qiu's men, who had been dispatched to murder Lin Chong and make it look like an accident. Lin Chong rushed out of the temple and slew the trio. Then he went off to join the rebels on Mount Liang.

## 婴 宁

《聊斋志异》中的故事。清朝，山东莒县有个王子服，14岁就中了秀才。17岁那年正月十五日，他到村外游玩，见一容貌美丽少女，手里拈着一枝梅花，满面笑容，一时看呆了。子服回家神魂颠倒，卧床不吃不喝，如患重病。表兄吴生见表弟如此，便撒谎道："你见那少女是你姨表妹婴宁，住在西南三十里的山中，还没有出嫁，我为你说媒去。"子服的病一下子就好了，他等不及表兄回话，就到姨母家，带回婴宁。母亲大吃一惊。她有个表姐，早死了，也没有女儿。只见婴宁貌美绝世，针线活做得精巧，笑起来娇媚可爱，周围人都感到快乐，就同意了儿子婚事。过一年，婴宁生了一个儿子，见谁都笑。婴宁告诉子服，她是狐仙的女儿。

## YING NING

THE STORIES BEHIND THE LONG CORRIDOR PAINTINGS AT THE SUMMER PALACE

This is a story from Strange Tales from the Make-Do Studio. In 1648, during the Qing Dynasty, 14-year-old Wang Zifu of Juxian County, Shangdong Province, passed the imperial examinations at county level. When he was 17 years old he saw a pretty girl holding a twig of plum blossoms and smiling at him. He fell in love with her, and when he was told that she was his cousin, went to his aunt's house. When he brought Ying Ning home, his mother was startled because her sister had died childless a long time previously. But when she saw Ying Ning's beauty, her excellent needlework, lovely smiles and pleasant personality, she agreed to the marriage. A year passed. Ying Ning gave birth to a son who smiled at everyone. Ying Ning eventually confessed that she was the daughter of a fox fairy.

## 画龙点睛

南北朝著名的大画家张僧繇擅画人物、动物，尤为画龙。
他画的龙形象逼真，呼之欲出。有人请他在金陵安乐寺
的墙壁上画了四条飞龙，皆无眼睛，观者问他为什么？
他说，要画上龙睛，龙就会破壁飞走。人们不信，说是
一派胡言，用笔画的龙怎么会飞呢？他无可奈何，举笔
点上一条龙的眼睛。刹那间，电闪雷鸣，有眼睛的龙，
破壁而出，在风雨中飞去。"画龙点睛"的成语也由此而
得。

## PAINTING IN THE PUPILS OF A DRAGON'S EYES

Zhang Sengyou (420-479), a famous painter of the Southern and Northern
Dynasties, excelled at painting human figures and animals, especially
dragons. Once he was invited to paint four dragons on the walls of the
Anle Temple in Jinling (today's Nanjing). After he had finished, people
saw that none of the dragons had pupils in their eyes, and asked him why.
Zhang Sengyou told them that the dragons would fly away from the walls
if he painted in the pupils of their eyes. As nobody believed him, Zhang
painted in the pupils of the eyes of one of the dragons. All at once, a
violent storm arose, and lightning flashed across the sky accompanied by
thunder. The dragon with pupils in its eyes detached itself from the wall,
and flew away in the storm.

## 傻大姐无意泄机关

《红楼梦》中的故事。贾母安排宝玉娶宝钗冲喜，又怕病中的宝玉和多病的黛玉闹出事来。王熙凤想出个掉包的法子。明里，告诉宝玉娶黛玉，外头人一概不许提起此事，瞒着黛玉。不料，贾母房里的傻大姐说开了："咱明儿更热闹了，又是宝姑娘，又是宝二奶奶，这可怎么叫呢！"傻大姐挨了一个大嘴巴，跑到外面去哭，偏偏碰上林黛玉，就一五一十地说了，还让林姑娘评理。黛玉知道此事后，迷迷糊糊地走回潇湘馆，身子往前一栽，一口血直吐出来。几天后，就在宝玉娶宝钗的时辰，黛玉喊着宝玉的名字气绝。

## NUMBSKULL CAN'T KEEP A SECRET

From A Dream of Red Mansions. Jia Baoyu and Lin Daiyu were lovers. When a marriage was arranged for Jia Baoyu with another girl, everybody was sworn to secrecy, for fear that Lin Daiyu, who was in poor health, would not be able to stand the shock. However, a feeble-minded servant girl nicknamed Numbskull blurted out the secret to Lin Daiyu. A few days later, while the wedding ceremony was being held, Lin Daiyu died, murmuring the name of Jia Baoyu.

## 韩康卖药

公元147 年，汉桓帝在位时，长安有个采药卖药的韩康，一个价钱卖药，三十年药价不变。"口不二价"的韩康，在长安可算人人皆知。一天，一个妇女前来买药，韩康出价，妇女讨价还价，韩康分文不让。妇女生气地说："难道你是口不二价的韩康不成？"顿时，韩康羞愧难言。他想，连妇女都知道他的坏名声，还有何脸面再卖药。便躲进深山隐居。桓帝听说这件事，觉得韩康这个人办事一丝不苟，便请他出山做官。他走到半道，觉得实在没脸见人，又回山去了。

## HAN KANG SELLS MEDICINAL HERBS

During the reign of Emperor Heng of the Han Dynasty (206 B.C.-220 A.D.) there was a man named Han Kang who picked medicinal herbs and sold them at the market in the capital, Chang'an. He sold all the herbs for the same price, which he kept unchanged for 30 years. One day, he demanded a higher price, and was scolded by a woman customer. Ashamed, he went into seclusion in the mountains. Emperor Heng heard about this incident, and was impressed by Han Kang's integrity. He offered Han Kang a position at court, but the latter refused.

## 三碗不过冈

《水浒传》中的故事。北宋末年，山东阳谷县地面有一家酒
店，挑着一面招牌在门前，上面写着三碗不过冈。一天，山
东好汉武松路过这里喝酒。店主人拿来三只碗，筛满三碗酒，
武松接连饮尽，连称："好酒！"他要店家再筛，主人不肯。
说是三碗就会醉倒，过不了这个景阳冈。武松不依，要打碎
这家酒店。主人怕他，为他筛完十八碗酒。武松喝完酒，绰
起哨棒，起身过冈。这才引出武松打虎景阳冈的故事。

## THREE BOWLS OF WINE BARS YOU
## FROM JINGYANG RIDGE

This is a story from Outlaws of the Marsh. At the end of the Northern
Song Dynasty, there was a wine shop in Yanggu County, Shandong
Province. In front of the gate hung a sign that announced: "No one
who has drunk three bowls of wine is allowed to cross Jingyang
Ridge." There was a tiger on the ridge, and the local authorities feared
that drunken travelers might fall prey to it. One day, Wu Song, on his
way to cross Jingyang Ridge, drank 18 bowls of wine here. Despite
the tavern keeper's protestations, he insisted on crossing the ridge.
Sure enough, he encountered the tiger, and killed it after a ferocious
battle.

## 陶渊明爱菊

"采菊东篱下，悠然见南山。"这首脍炙人口的诗句，至今仍在中国广泛流传。由此也引出晋代大诗人陶渊明爱菊的传说，陶渊明的祖辈都曾为官。陶渊明从小受书香门第的熏陶，博览群书，但受老子、庄子思想影响较深，虽然也曾几次做官，但厌倦官场上的周旋，热爱自然，最终辞官回乡，过着归田隐居的生活。"采菊东篱下"的全诗如下：

> "结庐在人境，而无车马喧。
> 问君何能尔？心远地自偏。
> 采菊东篱下，悠然见南山。
> 山气日夕佳，飞鸟相与还。
> 此中有真意，欲辨已忘言。"

## Tao Yuanming Loves Chrysanthemums

Tao Yuanming, a leading poet of the Eastern Jin Dynasty (317-420) was highly educated, but forsook officialdom for a life of seclusion. One of his most famous nature poems goes:
"Among the haunts of men I build my cot,
There's noise of wheels and hooves, but I hear not.
How can it leave upon my mind no trace?
Secluded heart creates a secluded place.
Picking chrysanthemums at the eastern twig fence,
Leisurely I look up and see the southern mountain,
Where mountain air is fresh both day and night,
And where I find home-bound birds in flight.
What is the revelation at this view?
Words fail me even if I try to tell you."

## 鲁智深大闹野猪林

《水浒传》中第八回故事。林冲被高俅陷害，刺配到沧州劳役。高俅又派人买通了押解差役董超、薛霸，在路上结果林冲。途经野猪林休息，二差役借口怕林冲逃走，将林冲绑在树上。二差役毒计得逞，举棍劈向林冲的脑袋。突然，林后飞出一条铁禅杖，将水火棍打到九霄云外，树后跳出一个胖大和尚。这和尚正是林冲在东京大相国寺交的朋友鲁智深。

## LU ZHISHEN SAVES LIN CHONG'S LIFE

From Outlaws of the Marsh. Having caused Lin Chong to be banished, Gao Qiu bribed the guards who were escorting him to kill him on the way. On the pretext of taking a rest, the guards tied Lin Chong to a tree. One guard raised his cudgel and aimed a blow at Lin Chong's head, when a fat monk suddenly appeared and defended Lin Chong with an iron shovel. The monk was Lu Zhishen, and he and Lin Chong became sworn brothers.

## 鲁智深倒拔垂杨柳

鲁智深原是渭州提辖，因路见不平，打死镇关西，逃遁在江湖，在五台山落发为僧，又被推荐到东京大相国寺管菜园。一日，他和园外东京泼皮饮酒，树上乌鸦吵个不停。众泼皮要上树拆除乌鸦窝。鲁智深走到树前，右手向下，把身倒缴着，却把左手拔往上截，把腰只一趁，将那株绿杨树带根拔起。又一日，鲁智深演练浑铁禅杖，忽听墙外喊好，他这才结交了林冲。

## LU ZHISHEN UPROOTS A WILLOW TREE

From Outlaws of the Marsh. Lu Zhishen had once been a minor official. He was enormously strong, and had to flee after killing a man. He became a monk at the Monastery of Great Assistance to the State. One day, while drinking with some others under a willow tree, they were disturbed by the cawing of crows in the tree. Lu Zhishen yanked the tree right out of the ground.

## 六子闹弥勒

中国民间传说。弥勒佛用后天袋子，又称＂人种袋＂，收服了六个童子，他们都是神通广大的人间妖怪。别看童子和弥勒佛之间关系亲密，但童子并不听话，一有机会便会跑到人间兴风作浪，弥勒佛还得费力气到人间收服。唐代李世民年间，一年三月初三，六童之一黄眉童子趁弥勒佛赴元始会，偷偷跑到人间，假扮如来佛祖，把唐僧一行取经人捉去，这是《西游记》中第六十六回的故事。

## FAKE BUDDHA CAPTURES XUANZANG

From Journey to the West. Maitreya, the Buddha of the Future, kept six demons imprisoned in a bag. One of them, the Yellow-Browed Lad, took advantage of Maitreya being away one day to sneak out of the bag and descend to Earth. Disguised as Buddha Tathagata, he captured the Tang Priest Xuanzang and his disciples as they were on their way to the West.

## 老黄忠

《三国演义》中的故事。公元220年，中国形成魏、蜀、吴三国对峙的局面。三方各自都想吞并对方。一日，魏军大将张郃引兵来打蜀地葭萌关。关上守军向成都告急求援。刘备请军师诸葛亮及众将到堂上议事。诸葛亮道："魏将张郃勇猛，非等闲可及。除非张飞，无人可当。"忽听一声喊道："军师为何轻视众人？"原来是老将黄忠，年近七十，出来请战。黄忠出马，用计大破张郃，又智夺曹军粮草，攻下定军山，大获全胜。"老将黄忠"也成为今天人们不服老的口头禅。

## OLD GENERAL HUANG ZHONG

From The Romance of the Three Kingdoms. During the wars between the kingdoms of Wei, Shu and Wu, the army of Wei, led by General Zhang He, attacked the Shu forces at Jiameng Pass. The king of Shu, Liu Bei, called a council of war, at which he asked for a volunteer to march against the doughty Zhang He. General Huang Zhong, at the time nearly 70 years old, stepped forward and asked for the assignment. Huang Zhong not only defeated Zhang He, he also seized the provisions of the army of Cao Cao, ruler of Wei and occupied strategic Dingjun Mountain. The name Huang Zhong later became synonymous with the pet phrase: "old but more vigorous".

## 许褚裸衣斗马超

《三国演义》中故事。西凉大将马超报杀父之仇，率二十万大军攻下长安，占领潼关。曹操手下大将于禁、张郃、曹洪都不是马超对手。潼关一战，曹操也险些被杀。曹操"虎卫军"头领许褚，人称"虎痴"，曾多次救曹操于危难之中，心中不服马超，出阵来战。两人交战一百余回合，不分胜负，但马匹脱力，各自换马再战。两人又杀了一百多回合，各自回阵换马。只见许褚卸了盔甲，赤体提刀出阵。马超一见，迎杀上去。马超艺高，许褚勇猛，在《三国演义》中是段精彩故事。

## XU CHU FIGHTS MA CHAO

From The Romance of the Three Kingdoms. Ma Chao, a general of the State of Western Liang, led 200,000 troops to seek revenge on Cao Cao for his father's death. They captured Chang'an and occupied Tongguan Pass. The battle between Cao Cao's general Xu Chu and Ma Chao forms one of the most exciting episodes in the novel. When the first 100 rounds resulted in a draw, they changed horses and fought another 100 rounds.

## 元春省亲

《红楼梦》中故事。荣国公贾政的大女儿元春被封为贵妃，恩准第二年元宵节回贾府省亲。贾府为此忙了起来。辟出三里半大小土地，堆山凿地，起楼竖阁，种竹栽花，采买女孩子，下姑苏聘请教习教戏，置办各种物品。一年后，园内崇阁巍峨，层楼高起，玉栏绕砌，金辉兽面，彩焕螭头。元春省亲当晚，园内各处帐舞蟠龙，帘飞彩凤，金银焕彩，珠宝争辉。见此景，元春也默默叹息奢华过费了。三百年后的今天，人们在北京仍然能看到大观园的情景。

## YUANCHUN PAYS A VISIT TO HER HOME

From A Dream of Red Mansions. Jia Yuanchun, the eldest
daughter of Jia Zheng, was made the highest-ranking imperial
concubine, and taken to live in the palace. At the Lantern Festival
the following year, she was allowed to pay a visit to her old
home. The Jia family built a special garden for her visit, with
rockeries, ponds, buildings and pavilions, and planted bamboo
groves and flowers. They also bought some girls and trained
them as singers and dancers to entertain Jia Yuanchun. The
garden took a year to construct. Three hundred years have
passed, but people still sigh with admiration when they visit the
Grand View Garden in Beijing.

## 穆桂英绝谷寻栈道

《杨家将》中故事。杨宗保已50岁，镇守西部边关，抗击西夏国对中原的不断骚扰。一日，边关紧急通报：杨宗保深入绝谷身亡，西夏国兵破边关，大举进攻中原。朝廷得知震惊，但无一人敢领兵抗敌。此时，佘太君已近百岁，带领孙媳穆桂英，重孙杨文广，全家出征，报家仇国恨。杨将奋勇杀敌，西夏兵溃不成军。宋兵追至山谷，正是宗保丧生处。在采药老人的指引下，穆桂英骑上宗保生前的坐骑，在绝谷中找到栈道，直插西夏军营，与祖母里应外合，歼灭了西夏军。

## MU GUIYING FINDS THE SECRET PLANK ROAD

From Generals of the Yang Family. During the Song Dynasty (960-1279), when Yang Zongbao, who had guarded a pass against encroachment by the State of Western Xia died, the latter captured the pass and launched a massive attack on the Central Plains. She Taijun, who was nearly 100 years old, took her grandson's wife Mu Guiying, her grand grandson Yang Wenguang, and other members of the Yang family and pushed back the Western Xia army. Guided by an old herb collector, Mu Guiying rode Yang Zongbao's old horse along a plank roadway through the narrow pass, straight on to the Western Xia camp, where she routed the enemy.

## 云萝公主

《聊斋志异》中的故事。从前，河北省卢龙县有一个叫安大业的书生，一生下来就会说话，长大后一表非凡，文才出众。一天大业正在读书，突然，一群婢女簇拥一位美丽少女走进书房，霎时间异香满屋，四壁生辉。原来是圣后府上的云萝公主下嫁大业、寻驸马来了。大业仓皇不知所为，随手取出棋子与公主对弈。大业棋术高明，乃人间高手，今日却接连输给公主。大业求公主结为百年之好，公主说："若为棋酒之交，可得三十年聚首；若作为夫妻，可六年谐合。"大业说："还是做夫妻，六年后再说今后的事。"六年里，公主为大业生有两男，离去。

## PRINCESS YUNLUO

From Strange Tales from the Make-Do Studio. Once upon a time there was a scholar named An Daye in Lulong County, Hebei Province. He was able to speak as soon as he was born. He grew up and turned out to be a handsome young man of unusual literary talent. One day, while An Daye was reading, a graceful young lady walked into his room accompanied by several maids. All at once, the room was filled with a strange fragrance and looked brighter. It was Princess Yunluo from the official residence of Shenghou, who had come to marry An Daye. The young man was at a loss. He started to play a board game with the princess. Despite being a master of the game, that day he lost one game after another to the princess. Princess Yunluo said: "I'll be with you for 30 years if we keep our relationship to the board game and cups of wine, but I'll be with you for only six years if we get married." An Daye said: "Let's get married now, and let the future take care of itself." The couple lived happily, and Princess Yunluo gave birth to two boys, and left at the end of the six years.

## 袭陈仓武侯取胜

《三国演义》中的故事。公元228年，东吴大败魏兵，并派使臣致书蜀中，请兵伐魏。诸葛亮上表出师，起三十万精兵，径奔陈仓道口而来。不料，陈仓口已筑起一城，内有魏将郝昭把守，深沟高垒，遍排鹿角。诸葛亮攻城二十余日，无计可破。忽报魏军千辆运粮车于祁山之西，运粮官乃孙礼。诸葛亮看破孙礼诱蜀军夺粮的计谋，派大将马岱引兵三千，于上风头放火烧车，车上硫黄焰硝燃起；又派二将各引五千人马在外围住。魏兵大败，孙礼引残兵突烟冒火而走。诸葛亮收军退回汉中，再谋陈仓。

## ZHUGE LIANG TAKES CHENCANG

From The Romance of the Three Kingdoms. In 228, the Kingdom of Wu inflicted a crushing defeat on the kingdom of Wei. Wu requested reinforcements from the Kingdom of Shu to finally crush the Wei Kingdom. Liu Bei, ruler of Shu, sent his commander Zhuge Liang with 300,000 picked troops to attack the Wei stronghold of Chencang. Unexpectedly, a strong fortress city had been built in front of Chencang and deep trenches dug around it. Hao Zhao, a general of Wei, guarded the city. Zhuge Liang attacked the city for over 20 days, but failed to take it. Suddenly someone reported to Zhuge Liang that there were thousands of Wei army carts of grain and forage to the west of Qi Mountain. Sun Li was the one in charge of transporting the grain and forage for the Wei army, and Zhuge Liang saw through Sun Li's scheme to lure the Shu army to take these supplies. He then ordered Ma Dai to take 3,000 men and set fire to the carts loaded with sulphur at the windward and sent two generals each leading 5,000 soldiers to encircle the enemies from outside. The Wei troops were utterly defeated. Sun Li had to flee out of the fire and smoke with the rest of his soldiers. Zhuge Liang recalled his troops to Hanzhong and made another plan to take Chencang.

## 寒塘鹤影

《红楼梦》第七十六回故事。中秋之夜，史湘云和黛玉来到凸碧堂下近水赏月。只见天上一轮皓月，池中一轮水月，上下争辉，引发二人的诗兴，便作起诗来。黛玉正吟到："壶漏声将涸"，突见池中黑影，湘云拾起一块小石向那池中打击，只听黑影里嘎然一声，飞起一个白鹤。湘云笑道："这个鹤有趣，倒助我了。"因联道："窗灯焰已昏。寒塘渡鹤影"，黛玉叫好，连说了不得。思索半天，对道："冷月葬花魂"。湘云拍手称道："果然好极！"这便是中秋夜大观园即景取句三十五韵中的佳句。

## A CRANE'S SHADOW ON A CHILLY POND

From Chapter Seventy-Six of A Dream of Red Mansions. On the night of the Mid-Autumn Festival, Shi Xiangyu and Lin Daiyu went to the Convex Emerald Hall to enjoy the moon. Seeing the bright full moon and its reflection in the water of the pond, the two were greatly inspired, and started to compose poems. They suddenly noticed a shadow on a nearby pond. Xiangyu threw a pebble at the shadow. Startled, a crane flew away. Xiangyu then continued the poem Daiyu had left unfinished: "The flame of the candle by the window is dim. A crane's shadow flits across the chilly pond."

## 牧童遥指杏花村

人们在清明时节踏青出游，不料细雨纷纷，下个不停。游人想寻一处乡间酒家，以便休息打尖，牧童告诉在杏花深处。图中画面就是根据唐代诗人杜牧的诗意绘成。原诗这样写道：

"清明时节雨纷纷，路上行人欲断魂。

借问酒家何处有，牧童遥指杏花村。"

这首朗朗上口的诗句，不仅中国古人喜爱，就是现代人也几乎人人会背诵。

## THE BUFFALO BOY
## POINTS OUT THE WINE SHOP

Painting based on a poem by Du Mu. Some people on a spring outing on the day of the Pure Brightness Festival were caught in the rain, and were eagerly seeking a tavern for shelter and refreshment. A local boy attending his buffalo pointed out a wine shop deep in an apricot grove. The poem is well known in China.

## 诸葛亮奇兵袭陈仓

且说诸葛亮上表出师，攻陈仓不下，却得胜退回汉中。一日，哨探来报："陈仓城中魏将郝昭病重。"诸葛亮说："大事成矣。"遂唤魏延、姜维两员大将，各领五千兵马，三日后起兵，星夜直奔陈仓城下，见火起攻城。令关兴、张苞点军，暗出汉中，星夜径到城下，早派细作在城内放火，发喊相助。郝昭病危，正在呻吟，忽报蜀军到城下，各门起火，城中大乱，惊吓而死，蜀兵一拥入城。诸葛亮明里派兵，隐人耳目；暗里出征，"出其不意，攻其不备"，轻取陈仓。

## ZHUGE LIANG TAKES CHENCANG BY A SURPRISE ATTACK

Zhuge Liang once submitted a memorial on going to war. Although the Shu army failed to capture Chencang, they defeated the Wei troops using fire and returned to Hanzhong. One day, a scout came to report, "Hao Zhao is seriously ill." Zhuge Liang said: "The chance has come." He ordered two generals Wei Yan and Jiang Wei to take 5,000 troops each, drive straight to Chencang in three days, and attack Chencang when they saw a fire inside the city. He then ordered Guan Xing and Zhang Bao to leave Hanzhong secretly for the city on the evening of that day. He asked the spy inside the city to start a fire to help the army outside the city. Hao Zhao was critically ill and groaning at the moment when he suddenly heard the report that the Shu army had arrived at the outskirts of the city and that all the gates of the city were on fire, which had thrown it into confusion. Hao Zhao was so frightened that he died on the spot. The Shu army marched into the city and took Chencang. Zhuge Liang sent troops to Chencang openly in order to hide his true intention, while ordering others to carry out his secret plans. He took Chencang easily by using the strategy of "taking the enemy by surprise and striking when it is unprepared."

## 红 玉

《聊斋志异》中故事。广平书生冯相如在夏夜里读书，忽听院墙有声，从上面下来一位美丽少女，名为红玉。两人一见钟情。从此，红玉每夜必来陪伴相如，如此半年有余。一天，被相如父亲发现，相如受责，红玉受辱后也不再来。之后，相如娶妻卫氏，又得一子叫福儿，日子过得倒也美满。一年清明节，卫氏随夫君祭祖扫墓，被当地劣绅看中。劣绅抢走卫氏，打死冯老翁，打伤相如，又将福儿扔进山谷。幸得红玉救起福儿，派人杀死劣绅，携福儿来见相如。相如悲喜交集。红玉告诉相如，她是狐仙，一直在暗中帮助他。

## HONG YU

From Strange Tales from the Make-Do Studio. Feng Xiangru, a scholar of Guangping, was reading one summer night when a beautiful girl named Hong Yu suddenly appeared. The two fell in love at first sight. From then on, Hong Yu visited the scholar every night for over half a year. One day, Xiangru's father found Hong Yu together with his son in his son's room, for which he strongly rebuked Xiangru. After this Hong Yu never came again.

Later, Xiangru married a woman from the Wei family, and before long they had a son named Fu'er. They lived happily and peacefully. One year, at the Pure Brightness Festival, the family went to pay their respects at the tombs of the ancestors of Xiangru's family. A wicked local squire had his men kidnap Xiangru's wife, beat Xiangru's father to death, injure Xiangru and throw Fu'er into a deep valley. Fu'er was rescued by Hong Yu, who ordered the squire killed, and restored Fu'er to Xiangru. It turned out that Hong Yu was a fox fairy, and that she had been watching Xiangru the whole time.

## 张敞画眉

公元前73年，汉宣帝登基，京都长安盗匪横行。豫州刺史张敞却毛遂自荐，愿调京城为官。张敞上任后，首先宴请盗匪头子，向他们示好；后大摆宴席，款待前来赴宴的众匪徒。待盗匪们酒酣耳热，一个个酩酊大醉时，张敞一声令下，埋伏在四周的刀斧手，一齐冲出，将数百名强盗一网打尽。张敞又开始惩治为非作歹的皇亲国戚。有人上本参他为妻子画眉，有失官体。宣帝查问此事，张敞说："夫妻间比画眉更风流的事还有呢，皇帝也一一查问？"宣帝听他说的有理，见他治理长安有功，就笑笑了事。

## ZHANG CHANG PUTS ON MASCARA FOR HIS WIFE

In 73 BC Emperor Xuan of the Han Dynasty ascended the throne. Robbers ran wild in Chang'an, the capital city, and Zhang Chang, the governor of Yuzhou Prefecture, recommended himself for the post of official in the capital city. After taking up the post, Zhang Chang's first step was to invite the chieftains of thieves and robbers to Chang'an to show his amiability to them. He then held a banquet for all thieves and robbers. After all of them had got drunk, Zhang Chang ordered his officers to take action, and several hundred thieves and robbers were captured. After that, Zhang Chang started to deal with evil-doers who were relatives or family members of high officials, one of which hated him and tried to find fault with him. They accused him of being frivolous and of disgraceful behavior as a high official as he put on mascara for his wife. When Emperor Xuan asked about this, Zhang Chang said: "There are far more amorous affairs than this between a married couple. Does your majesty intend to hear them one by one?" Realizing that he said was quite reasonable, and bearing in mind his merits and achievements in putting Chang'an in order, the emperor simply smiled and let it go.

## 高衙内戏林娘子

《水浒传》中第七回故事。太尉高俅义子花花太岁在岳庙五岳楼下遇见林冲妻子，上前调戏，被林冲冲散，心中着迷林娘子，整日里郁郁不乐。他手下人富安献计，买通林冲朋友陆谦，请林冲到外面吃酒。富安又慌慌急急奔到林冲家中，谎报林冲在陆谦家中一口气上不来倒下了。林娘子被带到陆家，高衙内正在那里等候，上前调戏。使女锦儿脱身寻得林冲，林冲三步做一步，跑到陆谦家。高衙内吃了一惊，开了楼窗，跳墙走了。从此，高衙内一病不起，高俅才定计害林冲。

## MASTER GAO TAKES LIBERTIES WITH LIN CHONG'S WIFE

This is a story from Chapter Seven of the Outlaws of the Marsh. Master Gao, the adopted son of Gao Qiu, ran into Lin Chong's wife at the Wuyue Building and took liberties with her. Lin Chong came and drove him away. Master Gao could not stop thinking of Lin Chong's wife and felt gloomy all day long. His subordinate Fu An made a suggestion. They bribed Lu Qian, a friend of Lin Chong, and told him to invite Lin Chong to drink at a wine shop. Then Fu An hurriedly ran to Lin Chong's home and lied to Lin Chong's wife, saying that Lin Chong had choked and collapsed in Lu Qian's home. Lin Chong's wife was led to Lu's home where Master Gao had been waiting for her. On seeing her arrive, Master Gao began to make advances towards her. The maid Jin'er ran away and found Lin Chong, who rushed to Lu's home. Master Gao was startled to see Lin Chong. He opened the window, jumped out of the building and ran away. Following this, Master Gao was seriously ill, which prompted Gao Qiu to work out a scheme to make Lin Chong the victim of a frame up.

## 珊 瑚

《聊斋志异》中的故事。四川重庆有个叫安大成的青年，弟弟二成，母亲沈氏。大成娶妻珊瑚，性情娴淑，母亲悍谬不仁，虐待珊瑚，并把珊瑚逐出家门。沈氏姐姐善视珊瑚，把珊瑚接到家中，靠纺纱度日。沈氏又为二成娶妻，名叫藏姑，性情暴戾，尤倍于婆婆，役使婆婆如婢女。沈氏病倒，惟有大成床前侍候，母子伤心哭泣。珊瑚听到婆婆病倒，用纺纱钱给婆婆买食物调养。沈氏病好了，得知是珊瑚孝敬自己，惭痛自挞，从此全家团圆。

## SHANHU

This is a story from Strange Tales from the Make-Do Studio. There was a young man named An Dacheng in Chongqing, Sichuan. He had a younger brother, An Ercheng, and a mother, Madame Shen. An Dacheng married Shanhu, who was a kind hearted and good tempered woman, but Dacheng's mother, Madame Shen, was irritable and fierce. She often ill-treated Shanhu and drove her out of the home. Madame Shen's sister was sympathetic toward her, and took Shanhu home and treated her well. Shanhu made a living from spinning yarn. Later Madame Shen arranged for her second son Ercheng to marry Zanggu, who was even fiercer than she was, and forced Madame Shen to work as a maid. Madame Shen eventually fell ill and only Dacheng came to her bedside to take care of her. The mother and son met and wept in grief. When Shanhu heard the news, she used the money she had made by spinning yarn and bought and prepared some food for Madame Shen. After Madame Shen recovered from her illness and learned that it was Shanhu who had been so filial and taken such good care of her she felt guilty and ashamed for the way she had treated Shanhu. They subsequently got together and lived a happy life.

## 嫦娥奔月

古时，天帝的10个儿子，即10个太阳，同时出来游玩，出现在天空上。没多久，地面江河干涸，大地干裂，树木枯死，禾苗枯焦。为了拯救地球生灵，天神羿带着妻子嫦娥来到人间。他力大无比，手举弓箭，一连射下9个太阳。地球又恢复了生机。可是羿得罪了天帝。天帝贬他们夫妻为凡人。嫦娥害怕死，羿又历经人间辛苦，长途跋涉，到昆仑山从王母处求来仙药。羿告诉嫦娥："这些药，两人吃了可以长生不死，一个人吃了可以飞升成仙。"嫦娥趁羿出门打猎，偷吃了全部仙药，飞升到暗不见天日的广寒宫，不敢见羿。

## CHANG'E FLIES TO THE MOON

In ancient times, the God of Heaven had ten sons. They often went out to play together and appeared in the sky as suns. Before long all the rivers dried up, the land cracked, and trees and crops withered. In order to save the people on earth, Hou Yi, an archer god, descended from heaven to earth with his wife. He had super strength and shot down nine of the ten suns. The earth came back to life again, but Hou Yi's actions had offended the God of Heaven, who reduced Hou Yi and his wife Chang'e to common people. Chang'e was afraid of death, so Hou Yi went through all manner of difficulties to get to Mount Kunlun and obtained the elixir of immortality from the Queen Mother of the West. Hou Yi told Chang'e, "If two people drink it together, they will live forever. If one person eats it all, he or she will ascend to heaven and become an immortal." One day while Hou Yi was out for hunting, Chang'e secretly drank all the elixir herself and flew up to heaven. She lived in the Palace of the Moon alone and dared not see Hou Yi again.

## 漂母分食待韩信

公元前206年，刘邦终于战胜了项羽，建立了汉朝。开国功勋淮阴侯韩信派人到处寻找一位老太太，送去千金，报答她当年分食之恩。原来，韩信小的时候专心学文习武，不懂得自食其力。由于父母过早谢世，他便在淮水岸边钓鱼换钱买吃的，生活很困难。淮水岸边有位老太太，为人家漂洗纱絮糊口，当地人称她为"漂母"。她见韩信钓不着鱼就挨饿，就把自己带的饭菜分一半给他吃。她天天如此，从不嫌弃韩信。"漂母"心地好，得到了好报。

## THE LAUNDRY WOMAN
## SHARES FOOD WITH HAN XIN

In 206 BC Liu Bang finally defeated Xiang Yu and set up the Han Dynasty. Han Xin, Marquis of Huaiyin and one of the founders, looked everywhere for an old woman and delivered to her one thousand pieces of gold in repayment for her sharing food with him in his early years. When Han Xin was young, he was absorbed in studying and practicing martial arts, and did not know how to earn his own living. As his parents had died earlier, he had to go fishing at the bank of the Huai River and sell the fish for food. At the riverside lived an old woman that made her living by taking in washing. The local people called her a "laundry woman". Seeing that Han Xin often went hungry when he failed to catch fish, the old woman started to share her meals with him every day and never tired of him. In the end her kindness was more than repaid.

## 五子夺魁

五代十国晚期，渔阳窦禹钧在朝为官，膝下有五子。窦禹钧教育他们刻苦读书，长大成才，不可虚度光阴。又请高师严加管教他们。随着五子年龄增长，家有万卷藏书，使他们博览古今。五子不负父望，相继中进士，连科及第，都做了高官。当时，五子全国闻名。后来，民间艺人以五子登科作为年画题材。春节到来，人们喜欢买回五子登科年画张贴。也有人买画赠送朋友，祝愿朋友孩子成才。

## THE FIVE SONS OF THE DOU FAMILY

During the late Five Dynasties (907-960), Dou Yujun, a court official at Yuyang, had five sons. He encouraged them to study hard, never to idle their time away and to be useful people in the future. He invited a learned tutor to teach his sons and instructed him to be strict. There was a rich collection of books in the Dou family, and as the children grew up, they all read these books and became learned men. They all passed the imperial examinations and were assigned posts as high officials. Their names became well known all over the country. Later, popular artists began to have their New Year's paintings based on the five sons of the Dou family who had passed the imperial examination. Before the Spring Festival, people like to buy New Year's paintings of the five Dou sons to paste on their walls or send to friends, thus wishing their children a successful future career.

## 姜太公钓鱼

商朝末期，有一位年逾古稀的老者姜子牙，每天垂钓在渭水之上。老者用无铒的直钓，高出水平三尺垂钓，嘴里还念念有词："负命者上钓来！"过往行人取笑于他，他却说："我名为垂钓，意不在鱼而在圣君。"文王听说此事，寻到渭水河边，找到了他。通过交谈，文王知道姜子牙有统兵、治国、安邦的才略，拜他为相。姜子牙辅佐文王，又辅佐武王灭了商纣，建立了周朝。

## LORD JIANG ANGLES FOR FISH

At the end of the Shang Dynasty in 11th century BC, lived an old man named Jiang Ziya, who went fishing every day by the Wei River. He used a straight hook without bait and let the line hover a meter above the water surface while murmuring: "The one who shoulders the responsibilities comes." All the passers-by laughed at him, but Jiang said: "My catch will not be a fish, but a wise ruler." Later King Wen of Zhou heard of this and came to look for him at the riverside. After talking with Jiang, King Wen learned that Jiang Ziya had a great talent for commanding the army and governing the country, and made him prime minister. Jiang Ziya helped King Wen and King Wu to overthrow the Shang Dynasty and establish the Zhou Dynasty.

## 米芾拜石

北宋年间，有一位性情古怪的大书画家，名叫米芾，又称"米氏云山"，因为他画山自成一家。他生平酷爱奇石，家中也多有收藏。每逢阴历单日清晨，他都要穿上朝服，参拜他所收藏的石头。他认为石头干净，参拜无知的石头胜过参拜他的上司贪官。一天，他到野外游玩，遇到一块巨大无比的奇石，便肃然起敬，连忙整理衣冠，伏首大拜。米芾拜石成为千古佳话，流传到今天。

## MI FU BOWS TO STONES

In the Northern Song Dynasty (960-1127) there was a great calligrapher with an eccentric character named Mi Fu. He was also called Cloudy Mountain of Mi, as the mountains he painted were distinctive. He was crazy about stones and had a huge collection at home. Every morning on odd-numbered days he would put on his official uniform and prostrate himself before the stones at home. He thought stones were clean and that it was better to bow to these innocent stones than his dirty and corrupt superiors. One day he went for an outing and saw a huge stone of a grotesque shape that evoked in him a feeling of profound respect. He arranged his clothes and hat and bowed deeply. This has become an often-told tale, passed on from generation to generation.

## 程颢泛舟

程颢，河南洛阳人，北宋时期的大哲学家，一生潜心研究理学，与其弟程颐二人是北宋的理学奠基人。阳春三月，他偶尔一次得闲，出来泛舟散心。时近中午，天蓝云淡，春风轻轻拂面。他望见沿河两岸杨柳垂青，春花烂漫，不觉沉醉在大自然美景之中。他一心贪看春天的景色，生怕路人把自己看成不务学业、一心贪玩的少年。随有感，写成《春日偶成》。

"云淡风轻近午天，傍花随柳过前川。

时人不识余心乐，将谓偷闲学少年。"

四句诗行勾勒成一幅美丽的图画。

## CHENG HAO GOES BOATING

Cheng Hao, born in Luoyang, Henan, was a famous philosopher of the Northern Song Dynasty. He was absorbed in the study of Neo-Confucianism all his life. He and his younger brother Cheng Yi were the founders of Neo-Confucianism in the Song Dynasty. One day in March when he was free, he went boating for some recreation. At noon the sky was blue and the spring breeze gently stroked his face. Glancing at the willows turning green and the flowers in bloom along the banks of the river, he was completely intoxicated by the beauty of nature. He had a passionate enjoyment of spring scenery, but feared others would mistake this for laziness. Therefore he wrote a poem "Impromptu Lines on a Spring Day":

"Towards noon beneath fleecy clouds and a gentle breeze,
I cross the stream amid blooms and willow trees.
Some strollers who do not know my heart's deep pleasure,
Would say I'm a truant fond of leisure."

The poem vividly illustrates the picturesque scenery of the time.

## 归田乐

描述东晋时期，著名诗人陶渊明《归去来辞》名篇的情景。陶渊明厌恶他13年的官场生涯，毅然挂印弃官，坐小船"舟遥遥以轻扬，风飘飘而吹衣"，要回到阔别已久的家园，心情激动，归心似箭，要过"悦亲戚之情话，乐琴书以消忧。采菊东篱下，悠然见南山"的田园生活了。

## PLEASURE AFTER RETIREMENT

This painting illustrates the scene described in the masterpiece The Ballad of Returning Home by Tao Yuanming, a famous poet in the Eastern Jin Dynasty (317-420). Tao Yuanming got tired of his 13 years as an official and gave up his post. He sat in a boat and felt "The boat was gently sailing and the wind lightly blowing through my clothes." He was excited and anxious to get back to his long-left home. He wanted to live an idyllic life where he would be "pleased to hear the caring words of relatives, cast care aside by listening to music and reading books, picking chrysanthemums at the eastern twig fence, and leisurely gazing at the southern mountain".

## 僧志南春日有诗

南宋时，年迈长髯的老人僧志南，迎着吹绿杨柳的春日
微风，不顾头上飘着杏花开时的绵绵细雨，扶杖走过东
去的小桥，径直奔向树荫下的小小游船，受春天的感染，
写下千古春天绝句：

　　　　"古木阴中系短篷，杖藜扶我过桥东；
　　　　沾衣欲湿杏花雨，吹面不寒杨柳风。"

## ZENG ZHINAN WRITES A POEM IN SPRING

In the Southern Song Dynasty (1127-1279) Zeng Zhinan, an old
man with a long beard, crossed a bridge heading east, using his
stick, towards a boat under a tree. He walked facing a spring
breeze that blew through the willow tree leaves, heedless of
showers, at a time when apricot trees were in blossom. He was so
inspired by the beauty of spring that he dedicated a lyrical poem
to this season:

　　　　"A small boat is fastened among the ancient trees.
　　　　I walk across the bridge to the east.
　　　　My clothes are soaked with apricot flower rain,
　　　　While the willow breeze stroking my face is not cold."

# 江 妃

相传在周朝，有个叫郑交甫的人，凭着花言巧语，占别人便宜。街坊邻居没有不指着他的脊梁骂他不仁的。这事不知怎么传到汉江中两位水仙江妃那里。一日，两妃乔装成美丽的少女在江面小舟上嬉戏，每人身上特意佩着一颗罕见的珍珠。郑交甫一见，顿生歹意，甜言蜜语还怕不足，竟唱起歌来要珍珠。两位少女把珍珠白送给他，他很快溜走。他手掌一直捂着衣兜里的珍珠不放，待他迫不及待地再看一眼时，珍珠竟不翼而飞，才明白自己被人戏弄了。

## JIANGFEI

In the Zhou Dynasty there was, according to legend, a man named Zheng Jiaofu. He would always try to take advantage of others by using fine words. All his neighbors would talk about him, complaining about his bad conduct. The Jiangfei, two narcissus fairies of Hanjiang, heard about Zheng by chance. One day, the two fairies disguised themselves as pretty girls playing in a boat on a river. Each wore a rare pearl to ornament their dress. Having seen the pearls, Zheng Jiaofu immediately came up with a plan of evil intent. He first tried all manner of flattery, but, fearing this insufficient for his purposes, began singing songs in order to win the pearls. The two girls gave them to him, upon which he promptly left. He kept the pearls in his palm, and his hand in his pocket. When he could wait no longer to see them and finally took his hand out of his pocket, the pearls had already disappeared. It was only then that he realized that he had been fooled.

## 天水关诸葛亮收服姜维

诸葛亮平定了南方，坐未安席，想到先帝刘备三顾草庐之恩，托孤之重；出师伐魏，兴复汉室。兵发天水关，破城之计被识破，大将赵云引蜀兵大败而回。诸葛亮闻听大吃一惊，方知此人名叫姜维，乃冀城人，事母至孝，文武双全，智勇足备。赵云又夸姜维枪法好。诸葛亮便亲自领兵抵天水城下，半夜又遭姜维袭击。诸葛亮认为姜维是真将才。想到欲传授平生之学，恨未得其人，姜维是他理想中传人。这才定计收服姜维。请看《三国演义》中第九十三回故事。

## ZHUGE LIANG WINS OVER JIANG WEI AT TIANSHUI PASS

That is a story from The Three Kingdoms. After Zhuge Liang conquered the South, he still could not rest. Remembering the kindness of former emperor Liu Bei who had paid him three visits at the thatched cottage, and the heavy responsibilities of taking care of Liu Bei's son, Zhuge Liang decided to send troops to suppress the Wei Kingdom and restore the Han court. He sent his troops to Tianshui Pass, but his strategy for conquering the city failed, and after suffering heavy losses General Zhao Yun took the Shu soldiers back. Zhuge Liang was astonished at this news, and soon learned that the one who had seen through his scheme was called Jiang Wei from Yicheng, who was a very filial son to his mother, as well as being intelligent and courageous, and good at martial arts and calligraphy. Even Zhao Yun praised Jiang Wei's excellent skill with spears. Zhuge Liang led troops to the city of Tianshui himself, and was attacked by Jiang Wei at midnight. Zhuge Liang then knew that Jiang Wei was an excellent general, and the ideal person to whom he should teach all the knowledge he had amassed. He therefore concocted a scheme to win Jiang Wei over.

## 陷空山无底洞

唐僧取经途经陷空山，被金鼻白毛老鼠精擒回三百里无底洞中。老鼠精识得唐僧乃童身修行，一点元阳未泄，拿他去配合，可成太乙金仙。她派小妖做些素果素菜筵席，要和唐僧成亲。她和唐僧携手挨背，交头接耳，做出千般娇态，万种风情，伸出尖尖之玉指，捧晃晃之金杯，满斟美酒，递与唐僧。正在这时，孙悟空来救唐僧。他变成老鹰，抡开玉爪，响一声掀翻桌席，唬得妖精心胆皆裂。这是《西游记》中第八十二回故事。

## BOTTOMLESS CAVE OF MOUNT PITFALL

This is a story from Chapter Eighty-Two of Journey to the West. The Tang priest was captured by the Golden Nosed White Haired Mouse Spirit and taken to her 150-kilometer-deep Bottomless Cave as he was passing Mount Pitfall on the way to the West to obtain Buddhist scriptures. The mouse spirit learned that the Tang Priest had practiced Buddhism since childhood and had never released his seminal fluid, and so thought she would become a golden immortal if she married him. She then ordered her little demons to lay on a banquet of fruit and vegetables that she and the Tang Priest would enjoy before she married him. The mouse spirit came to the Tang Priest, helped him to his feet, held his hand, stood with her side pressed against his as she whispered in his ear. She used her charm and tried every way to seduce him. Revealing the tips of her jade fingers she raised a dazzling golden goblet filled with fine wine and handed it to the Tang Priest. Just at this moment Monkey arrived to save the Tang Priest. He turned into an eagle, swung his jade claws and noisily overturned the tables. The mouse spirit was so terrified that her heart and gall bladder split open.

## 先天八卦图

八卦分为先天和后天八卦之说。先天八卦，即伏羲。宋代学者周敦颐根据《说卦传》和《系辞上传》创作了先天八卦图。先天八卦图序是：

乾一，兑二，离三，震四，
巽五，坎六，艮七，坤八。

图为周敦颐晚年讲先天八卦图的情景。

## THE INNATE EIGHT DIAGRAMS' CHART

The eight diagrams can be divided into inherent and acquired. The innate eight diagrams are also called Fu Xi's eight diagrams. Zhou Dunyi, a scholar of the Song Dynasty created the chart of the innate eight diagrams based on the books, "On Diagrams" and "Part One on Ballad." This painting depicts Zhou Dunyi giving his explanations of the chart of innate eight diagrams in his later years.

## 松下问童子

引之唐代诗人贾岛（779～843年）的《访隐者不遇》诗中第一句。这首诗也是唐诗三百首之一，已译成多种文字，在世界上广泛流传。贾岛这首诗，字简意明，短短二十个字，表达了人物、风景、事情的始末。

> "松下问童子，言师采药去，
> 　　只在此山中，云深不知处。"

图中画面正是诗的含意。

## ASKING A CHILD ABOUT A RECLUSE UNDER A TREE

This painting is based on the first line of a poem "A Note Left for An Absent Recluse" written by Jia Dao (779-843), a poet of the Tang Dynasty. This poem is also one of the three hundred poems of the Tang Dynasty. It has been translated into many languages and is known all over the world. The poem is very short with only 20 words, but it clearly depicts human figures, landscape and a story:

> "Asking a child about a recluse under a tree,
> The child said that his master went for herbs.
> He is surely in the mountains,
> But no where can be seen because of the thick clouds."

The painting clearly implies the meaning of the poem.

## 宴长江曹操赋诗

曹操平定了北方，又得荆襄九郡，计点马步、水军八十三万，水陆并进，船骑双行，沿江而来，要南渡长江，消灭孙权和刘备。公元208年农历十一月十五日，曹操令置酒设乐于大船之上。天色将晚，东山月上。曹操坐大船之上，左右侍御者数百人。文武众官，各依次而坐饮酒。饮至半夜，曹操酒酣已醉，取槊立于船头上作起歌来，这才留下了千古名句。现代人一开口，也能说上二句曹操歌词：

> "对酒当歌，人生几何？
> 譬如朝露，去日苦多。
> ……"

这是《三国演义》中第四十八回故事。

## CAO CAO SINGS AN ODE AT A FEAST ON THE YANGTZE RIVER

This is a story from The Three Kingdoms. After suppressing the separatist forces in the north and taking control of nine prefectures, Cao Cao led his 830,000 troops to the north bank of the Yangtze River, aiming to cross the river to destroy Sun Quan and Liu Bei who were on the other side. On the fifteenth day of the eleventh month of the Chinese lunar year in 208, Cao Cao ordered a feast and entertainment to be held on a large ship. It was getting dark as the moon climbed over the eastern mountains. Aboard ship, Cao Cao was surrounded by hundreds of generals. All the civil and military officials were seated in order, and by midnight Cao Cao was in his cups. He took out his spear, set it in the prow of the ship and began to sing an ode which was later to become famous, Even today people can recite its first two lines, "Here before us, wine and song! For man does not live long. Like daybreak dew, His day are swiftly gone."

## 水莽草

《聊斋志异》中的故事。湖北桃花江一带，生长着一种毒草，名为水莽草。人误食后身亡，变成水莽鬼，只有诱使别人食此草身亡，才能找到替身。少年祝生，出门访友。在一茶棚，见一少女姿容艳绝，给他倒茶。祝生一时迷恋女色，不知水莽草的异味。来到朋友家，他觉得心头作恶。朋友告知他喝了水莽草了。此女定是寇三娘，数年前误食水莽草而死。祝生咬牙切齿地说："我死后必不让此女脱生。"祝生急回家，到家门而死，变成了水莽鬼，把已投生的寇三娘强捉来为妻，又带着妻子回到人间侍候母亲，直到十余年后母死。他孝母有功于人世，天帝封他为四条大河的水神。

## HUGE WATERWEEDS

This is a story from Strange Tales from the Make-Do Studio. In the Taohua River area in Hubei there grew a kind of poisonous weed called the huge waterweed. People who ate it by accident would die and turn into huge waterweed monsters. They were unable to revert to human form until they lured others to eat the weeds and replace them. One day, a young man named Zhu Sheng went to visit a friend. He saw a beautiful girl in a tea shed pouring him a cup of tea. He was immediately infatuated by her charm and did not notice the strange smell of the huge waterweed. When he arrived at his friend's home, he felt nauseous. His friend told him that he had eaten the huge waterweed and that the girl was Kou Sanniang for sure, because she had died of eating the weeds by accident several years ago. Zhu Sheng declared, gnashing his teeth, "I will never let her get away with this after I die." Zhu Sheng rushed back home, and soon died and turned into a huge waterweed monster. He seized Kou Sanniang who had already changed back to human form and forced her to marry him. Then he took her back to the mortal world to look after his mother till she died ten years later. As he had performed meritorious service by showing filial respect to his mother, the God of Heaven conferred upon him the title of God of the Water of Four Rivers.

## 唐僧路阻火焰山

唐僧师徒四人取经赶奔西天。时值三秋霜景，却觉热气蒸人。原来前面有座火焰山阻路。一打听，得知火焰山八百里火焰，四周围寸草不生。要过此山，只有去翠云山芭蕉洞求铁扇公主，借来芭蕉扇灭火。那芭蕉扇本是昆仑山后，从混沌开辟以来，天地产生的一个灵宝，乃太阴之精叶，故能灭火气。可是铁扇公主是圣婴大王红孩儿的母亲，牛魔王之妻，要借扇得先降服牛魔王。图中孙悟空、猪八戒和沙和尚共斗牛魔王。这是《西游记》中第五十九回故事。

## TANG PRIEST IS STOPPED
## BY THE FLAMING MOUNTAINS

This is a story from Chapter Fifty-Nine of Journey to the West. The Tang Priest and his three disciples were on their way to the West for scriptures. It was autumn, but they felt it was getting hotter and hotter. Soon they realized that the Flaming Mountains stood ahead of them. They then learned that the flames of the mountains covered an area of 400 kilometers on which not a blade of grass could grow. If they wanted to cross the mountains, they would need to borrow a special plantain fan from Princess Iron Fan who lived in the Plantain Cave of Cuiyun Mountain. The plantain fan was a treasure created by heaven and earth after the earth separated from heaven. It was made from the spirit leaf of the sun, so it could extinguish fire. Princess Iron Fan was the mother of Red Boy and the wife of the Bull Demon King. They were required to suppress the Bull Demon King if they wanted to borrow the iron fan. This painting illustrates the scene of Monkey, Pig and Friar Sand in a fierce struggle with the Bull Demon King.

## 草船借箭

一日，周瑜请诸葛亮监造十万枝箭，十日完成。诸葛亮说只消三日，并立下生死军令状。第一、二天诸葛亮不动。第三日三更天，诸葛亮出动轻快船二十只，各船三十人，并布幔束草。五更天的时候，船近曹操水寨。诸葛亮教把船只头西尾东，一带摆开，就船上擂鼓呐喊。曹操传令："重雾迷江，不可轻动。拨水军旱寨万名弓弩手射箭。待至日高雾散，二十只船两边束草上排满箭枝，足有十万五千枝箭。诸葛亮令收船急回，曹操追之不及，懊悔不已。这是《三国演义》中第四十六回故事。

## BORROWING ARROWS WITH THATCHED BOATS

This is a story from Three Kingdoms. One day, Zhou Yu asked Zhuge Liang to supervise the manufacture of 100,000 arrows and have them completed within ten days. Zhuge Liang said that three days was sufficient time, and signed a pledge acknowledging his liability for punishment if he failed. Zhuge Liang did nothing for the first and second days. At midnight of the third day Zhuge Liang led twenty boats out, each lined with straw-made scarecrows and manned by thirty soldiers. Just before dawn the boats came close to Cao Cao's encampment. Zhuge Liang ordered all the boats to turn their bows to the west and sterns to the east and spread out in a line. Then he told the soldiers in the boats to beat drums and shout. Cao Cao said: "The fog is heavy on the river. We should not act rashly." He dispatched tens of hundred thousand bowmen to shoot arrows at the boats. When day broke and the fog lifted, the scarecrows on the twenty boats were shot full of arrows, about 150,000 in total. Zhuge Liang quickly ordered his men to withdraw. Cao Cao could not catch them and was deeply angered.

## 秦香莲

北宋年间，荆州秀才陈士美进京赶考，中了状元，被招为驸马，却忘了妻子秦香莲，也忘了高堂父母和一双儿女。数年后，陈士美父母在灾荒中病逝。秦香莲带着儿女上京寻夫，一直寻到京城驸马府。陈士美不认妻子儿女，秦香莲被逼无奈，挡住当朝丞相王延龄的轿子喊冤。这年八月十六日，是陈士美的生日。王丞相带着假扮歌女的秦香莲为陈士美祝寿。秦香莲弹起琵琶，唱起往日夫妻情深，家中不幸和苦难的日子。图中正是秦香莲弹唱祝寿的情景。

## QIN XIANGLIAN

In the Song Dynasty (960-1279) Chen Shimei from Jingzhou, who passed the imperial examination at county level, went to the capital to take the imperial examination at a high level. He won first place, and it was arranged that he should marry the emperor's daughter. He soon forgot his wife Qin Xianglian, his parents, and his son and daughter. Several years later, Chen's parents died of illness in a famine. Qin Xianglian went all the way to the capital with her children to look for her husband. She found him in the Emperor's Son-in-law Residence, but Chen Shimei refused to acknowledge her and his children. Qin Xianglian had no other recourse but to stop Wang Yanling, prime minister of the court, in his sedan chair, and pour out her grievances. The sixteenth day of the eighth month of the year was Chen's birthday. Prime Minister Wang brought Qin Xianglian, disguised as a singsong girl, to Chen's home to celebrate Chen's birthday. Qin Xianglian played the pipa and sang of their past love, and the misfortunes and hard life she suffered after he left. This painting illustrates the scene of Qin Xianglian celebrating Chen's birthday by singing to a pipa.

## 水淹七军

公元195年秋，刘备进位汉中王。曹操大怒，发誓要灭刘备。诸葛亮授计让关云长先出兵攻打樊城。樊城守将曹仁急差人求救。曹操派于禁为将军，庞德为先锋，大起七军，驰援樊城。关云长与庞德大战中中冷箭，把住隘口不出。于禁将七军移到樊城北十里罾口川，依山下寨。时值八月，骤雨数日，襄江水泛涨。关云长派人堰住各处水口。一夜，风雨大作，各处水口一齐放水，平地水深一丈，七军随波逐浪，于禁、庞德被擒。这是《三国演义》中第七十四回故事。

## FLOODING SEVEN ARMIES

This is a story from The Three Kingdoms. In the year 195 Liu Bei was given the title King of Hanzhong. Cao Cao was enraged and swore to destroy Liu Bei. Zhuge Liang confided a stratagem to Liu Bei to make Guan Yunchang attack Fancheng City. Cao Ren, the defending general of the city, immediately sent for help. Cao Cao ordered Yu Jin to be general and Pang De to be the vanguard of seven armies of reinforcements. Guan Yunchang was wounded by a sniper's shot in a battle with Pang De. He held the pass and did not come out to fight again. Yu Jin moved the seven armies to Zengkou Valley five kilometers north of the city and camped by the side of the mountain. This was in August, when there was heavy rain that lasted for days and caused the Xiangjiang River to rise swiftly. Guang Yunchang had his men dam up several points in the river. On one night of a particularly heavy storm, water was suddenly released from the dam and the floodwater reached a depth of three meters on the ground. The seven armies were soon washed away by floods, and Yu Jin and Pang De were soon captured.

## 细 柳

京都女柳少慧，腰细婀娜可爱，人们戏呼"细柳"。细柳喜读相书，相夫甚多，都说不行。十九岁时，听父母之命，嫁给丧妻遗子的高生。年余，生有一子，取名高怙。村中有卖好寿材的，细柳不惜重金购买。高生二十五岁时，不幸死去，一切备用齐全。遗子高福十岁，娇惰不肯读书，细柳让他换上破衣，与僮仆一起放猪，一起吃粗饭。高福吃尽苦头方知悔改。细柳让他重新读书。二子高怙读书笨，细柳让他务农，他偷懒；让他经商，他赌钱嫖娼；给他假金子事发，受尽了牢狱之苦，才把他救出。又三年，高福登第中进士，高怙务农持家，乡亲们才明白细柳是真心爱子。

## XILIU

Once upon a time there was a charming and lovely girl named Liu Shaohui. As she had such a tiny waist, people called her "Xiliu," meaning her waist was as slender as a willow branch. Xiliu was fond of reading books on physiognomy. She had met several men, but none that she had liked. At the age of nineteen she obeyed her parents' arrangements and married Gao Sheng, who had just lost his wife and had a son named Gao Hu. One year later she gave birth to a son and named him Gao Hu. As long as she could find good wood for making coffins, she would buy it, no matter how high the cost. So everything was ready when Gao Sheng died at the age of twenty-five. Gao Fu was pampered and spoiled, and had no wish to study at the age of ten. Xiliu made him wear shabby clothes and herd pigs and eat simple food with the houseboys. Gao Fu endured untold sufferings and finally decided to repent his errors, and Xiliu allowed him study again. Gao Hu, Xiliu's second son, was a slow-witted child, so Xiliu made him work in the fields, but Gao Hu was lazy and often neglected the work. Xiliu let him engage in business, but Gao Hu spent all his money on gambling and whoring. Xiliu then gave him fake gold to use, which put him in prison. Gao Hu suffered a lot in prison and was finally released. Three years later, Gao Fu became a successful candidate in the highest imperial examinations, and Gao Hu stayed at home and took care of the farm work. Fellow villagers then began to realize that Xiliu really loved her sons.

## 盗仙草

《白蛇传》中的故事。一条得道成仙变成人形的白蛇，名为白娘子，在杭州西湖的游船上，遇到书生许仙。二人一见钟情，结为了百年之好。第二年，迎来了五月初五端阳节。家家户户门上插艾叶，喝雄黄酒，吃粽子。蛇怕雄黄，但白娘子不得不过人间节日，陪丈夫喝了一口雄黄酒，显露了原形，吓死了许仙。白娘子酒醒后去昆仑山盗灵芝仙草，一心救活许仙。守山白鹤仙和鹿仙发现了她，打斗起来。此时，南极仙翁回山，白娘子向他求救。仙翁同情白蛇，送她仙草去救丈夫。白蛇传的故事在中国家喻户晓。

## STEALING MAGIC FUNGUS

This is a story from the Tale of the White Snake. A white snake attained the Way and turned into a woman named Lady Bai. She met Xu Xian, a scholar, in a pleasure-boat on the West Lake. They fell in love at first sight and married. The following year at the Dragon Boat Festival every household hung up Chinese mugwort, drank realgar wine, and ate Zongzi, a pyramid-shaped dumpling made of glutinous rice wrapped in bamboo or reed leaves. A snake is afraid of realgar wine, but Lady Bai had to celebrate the festival with her husband as every other household did. She accompanied her husband and drank a cup of wine. She then revealed her true identity and frightened Xu Xian to death. After Lady Bai woke up, she went to Mount Kunlun for the magic fungus that would save the life of Xu Xian. She was discovered by the crane guard and deer spirits, and they fought fiercely. At that moment the South Pole God returned, and Lady Bai begged him for help. The god sympathized, and gave her the fungus that would save her husband. This story is widely known in China.

## 穷不卖书留子读

从公元518年隋朝起，至清代止，中国许多读书人靠科举做官为出路，通过十年寒窗寻求出头的日子。但考中出头的人毕竟是少数，大多数读书人必定会名落孙山。几代人读书，无一考中的家庭普遍存在；但藏书却越来越多，家境越来越贫寒。可是落第的老人总是期待子孙连科及第，有时忍饥挨饿也不愿卖书买粮食吃。因此，就留下了"穷不卖书留子读，老米栽竹有人砍"的谚语。

## NEVER SELL BOOKS, EVEN IN POVERTY, BUT KEEP THEM FOR CHILDREN

From the Sui Dynasty in 518 to the Qing Dynasty in 1906, many Chinese people succeeded in becoming officials by passing the imperial examinations. They would spend ten years in intense study, waiting for the day to come, but only a small number succeeded in passing the examinations. The large majority of candidates would fail, and it was common for several generations of a family not to pass these examinations. Even so many families kept on collecting books that made them poorer and poorer, as the elders who had failed always hoped that their children or grandchildren could succeed one day. They preferred to endure the torments of hunger, rather than sell books for food, hence the proverb, "Never sell books even in poverty, but keep them for children; Planting bamboo trees at an old age is for someone to cut in the future." came into the usage.

## 《打渔杀家》

中国传统剧目之一。故事发生在北宋末年。萧恩老人和女儿桂英相依为命，靠打渔为生。这年天旱少雨，河浅鱼稀。渔霸丁子燮照例收萧恩的渔税，并动手打人。萧恩一气打跑了丁家家奴，并到县衙告丁家欺民。县官早已受丁子燮贿赂，不由分说，便当场打萧恩四十大板，打得萧恩皮开肉绽，还责令他向丁家赔罪。萧恩忍疼回家，让女儿带上礼品，暗藏戒刀，连夜奔丁家而来。丁子燮见萧恩父女献宝珠赔罪，心中得意。萧恩父女突然拔出戒刀，杀了丁子燮。

## THE FISHERMEN KILL THE DESPOT

This is a traditional opera piece. The story takes place in the late Northern Song Dynasty. The old man Xiao En and his daughter Guiying were dependent on each other and lived by fishing. One drought year the level of all river water dropped and fish were few. The fishing despot Ding Zixie came to collect taxes as usual and beat the old man. Xiao En got angry, and drove Ding's men away and went to court to sue them. Having been bribed by Ding Zixie, the magistrate did not listen to the old man and sentenced him to forty lashes. The poor man was bruised and lacerated and was ordered to apologize to Ding. Xiao En went back home, and in great pain asked his daughter to take some presents in which daggers were hidden. They went to Ding's home that night. Seeing Xiao En and his daughter come to apologize to him, bringing precious pearls, Ding Zixie was overjoyed. Suddenly, Xiao En and his daughter took out their daggers and killed Ding Zixie.

## 彭二挣

《聊斋志异》中故事。山东禹城县彭二挣与同村韩公甫一块去买东西。两人骑在驴上一前一后，边走边谈。走着走着，韩公甫听不见二挣讲话，回头一看，不见二挣，却隐约听到二挣的驴背口袋里发出急促的呼救声。韩公甫见二挣口袋缝得甚密，用刀断线，见二挣蜷卧其中。二挣说："我家里闹狐，此类事经常发生。"

## PENG ERZHENG

This is a story from Strange Tales of the Make-Do Studio. Peng Erzheng in Yucheng County, Shangdong, went out with Han Gongpu from the same village to buy a few things. They each rode a donkey and chatted along the way. Suddenly Han Gongpu could not hear Peng Erzheng speaking, and on turning his head, found that Peng had disappeared. He then heard Peng's faint cries for help from within a sack on the back of the donkey. Han Gongpu cut open the sack with a knife and saw Peng crouching inside. Peng said: "I've got fox troubles at home. Such a thing happens frequently."

## 断桥亭

《白蛇传》中故事。白娘子与许仙在镇江开了一家"保和堂"药店。这年，流行瘟疫，人们都到保和堂抓药。说来神奇，真是药到病除。金山寺法海和尚火冒三丈。他是有意散毒，好让患者去金山寺烧香，显示他的法力。法海用计，将许仙诓到金山寺，说白娘子就是蛇妖。许仙害怕，躲在寺中不出。白娘子非常着急，为救丈夫，引来大水，"水漫金山寺"，因身怀六甲，战法海不下，败下阵来，在西湖断桥亭遇上从寺里逃出的许仙。丫鬟小青恨许仙无情无义，举剑便刺。白娘子念夫妻之情，原谅了许仙。

## THE BROKEN BRIDGE PAVILION

This is a story from Tale of the White Snake. Lady Bai and Xu Xian opened a drugstore called "Baohetang". That year, the city was plagued with a seasonal febrile disease. All the people went to Baohetang drugstore for the medicine that helped them to recover rapidly. Monk Fahai of the Jinshan Temple was irritated, as he had spread the disease on purpose with the intention of inducing people to come to burn joss sticks at his temple, in order to show his power. He then worked out another vicious scheme and lured Xu Xian to his temple. He told Xu Xian that Lady Bai was a snake spirit. Xu Xian was alarmed, and hid himself in the temple. Lady Bai was deeply worried, and brought water to flood the temple. As she was pregnant, she could not win over Monk Fahai and retreated in defeat. She met Xu Xian, who had fled from the temple, at the Broken Bridge Pavilion. Xiao Qing, Lady Bai's maid, angrily held up her sword and was about to kill Xu Xian, but Lady Bai stopped Xiao Qing and forgave Xu Xian for the sake of their past happy matrimonial life.

## 关云长过五关斩六将

《三国演义》中第二十七回故事。刘、关、张被曹操大兵冲散。关云长为保护刘备二位夫人，暂时降了曹操。曹待云长三日小宴，五日大宴，送金银无数，美女十人，又上表封云长为汉寿亭侯。当关云长得知刘备消息后，将金银封置库中，悬汉寿亭侯印于堂上，抛美女于原处，保护二夫人而去。路经东岭杀了守将孔秀，过洛阳斩了太守韩福和牙将孟坦，经汜水关刀劈大将卞喜，过五关斩六将，与义兄刘备会合。图为卞喜手持流星锤与关云长厮杀情景。

## GUAN YUNCHANG SLAYS SIX GENERALS AND BREACHES FIVE PASSES

This is a story from The Three Kingdoms. Liu Bei, Guan Yuchang and Zhang Fei were separated by Cao Cao's troops. Guan Yuchang surrendered to Cao Cao temporarily in order to save the lives of two of Liu Bei's ladies. Cao Cao treated Guan Yunchang very well with a feast every three days and a banquet every five days. He also sent him a large amount of silver and gold and ten beautiful girls. Cao Cao also conferred on him the title of lord of Hanshou precinct. When Guan Yunchang heard of Liu Bei's whereabouts, he locked away all the gold and silver he had received, hung the seal of the lord of Hanshou precinct in the hall, and returned the ten beautiful girls. He then escorted the two ladies back to Liu Bei. On the way he killed the guarding general Kong Xiu at Dongling Pass, slew Han Fu and Meng Tan in Luoyang, and sliced general Bian Xi in two with his blade. After slaying six generals and breaching five passes, Guan Yunchang was finally reunited with his sworn brother Liu Bei. This painting illustrates the scene of Bian Xi holding his iron missiles in the fight with Guan Yunchang.

## 枪挑小梁王

《岳飞传》中的故事。南宋年间，朝延举行武科举，比文才、射箭、武功，选拔武状元。岳飞来到京都汴梁，下校场同一个叫柴桂的武举子最后比试。此人人称小梁王，身世显贵，文武双全，又用钱贿赂了主考官——丞相张邦昌。岳飞的《枪论》文章，九

## THROWING PRINCE XIAOLIANG DOWN FROM HIS HORSE

This is a story from The Complete Biography of Yue Fei. During the Southern Song Dynasty (1127-1279), the imperial court held a martial arts competition to select the best exponent of martial arts. All those attending competed in literary talent, archery, and martial arts. Yue Fei came to Bianliang, the capital city, and competed with Chai Gui in the final test. Chai Gui was also known as Prince Xiaoliang. He was the descendent of a high official family, and good at both writing and swordsmanship. In order to win the competition, he bribed the chief examiner, the prime minister Zhang Bangchang. Yue Fei's essay, "On the Spear," and his archery skills,

箭射透靶心的"箭法"，都高过小梁王。马上比武开始，小梁王手持
大刀，左抡右砍。岳飞是平常武生，有所顾忌，只是招架。几个回
合，岳飞拨马来到监考台前，要求立下"生死文书"。二人立书后上
马再战。岳飞银枪闪动，刺中小梁王心窝，将他挑下马来。全场喝
采。张邦昌要斩岳飞，岳飞的结拜兄弟牛皋四人冲进校场，砍倒大
旗，场内大乱，他们救起岳飞而走。

when all nine of arrows hit the bull's eye, were indubitably better than those of
Prince Xiaoliang in the first and second tests. At the start of the third test,
Prince Xiaoliang brandished his blade at Yue Fei who, afraid of hurting him,
merely dodged the prince's attack. After a few rounds, Yue Fei went up to the
examiners and asked to write a "life-and-death document". The two both wrote
the document and restarted the competition. Yue Fei attacked Prince Xiaoliang
with his spear, stabbed him in the heart and threw him down from his horse.
Yue Fei won the applause of the audience. Zhang Bangchang wanted to kill
Yue Fei, but at this moment, Niu Gao, Yue Fei's sworn brother, and other three
friends rushed into the drill ground. They chopped down the flag and, amid the
confusion, helped Yue Fei out of danger.

## 竹林七贤

魏末晋初，有七位老人，经常到一处山后竹林里饮酒、抚琴、作画、吟诗、对弈。他们是当代文人名士，名叫阮籍、嵇康、阮咸、山涛、向秀、王戎、刘伶，都在魏、晋两朝做过官。人们称他们为竹林七贤。

## SEVEN SAGES OF THE BAMBOO GROVE

At the end of the Wei Dynasty and at the beginning of the Jin Dynasty in 260-300, there were seven old men who often went to drink, play the pipa, paint, and chant poems in a bamboo grove behind a mountain. They were the seven outstanding literary men of the time named Ruan Ji, Ji Kang, Ruan Xian, Shan Tao, Xiang Xiu, Wang Rong and Liu Ling. They all served as officials at the Wei and Jin courts. People liked to call them the seven sages of the bamboo grove.

## 好洁成癖

在元朝，江苏无锡有位叫倪瓒的著名画家，擅画山水，并取各家画派之长，独创一家，为元代"元四家"之一。倪瓒爱画梧桐，便命人在书房四周栽上梧桐树。为了树身清洁，他每天早上都指使书童们汲水擦洗树身，并在一旁监督，直到他认为树身洁净为止。人们笑他迂腐，他不在意，每天仍然让书童洗树不止。史书上也说他"好洁成癖"。

## AN OBSESSION WITH CLEANLINESS

During the Yuan Dynasty (1206-1368) there lived in Wuxi a famous painter named Ni Zan. He was good at landscape paintings and created his own style by learning from others' good points. He was known as one of the "Four Schools of the Yuan Dynasty." Ni Zan was fond of painting the Chinese parasol tree. He ordered people to plant Chinese parasol trees around his study, and in order to keep the tree trunk clean, he made his page boys fetch water and wash the trunks every morning while he stood aside supervising them till the trunks were cleaned to his satisfaction. People all laughed at him for his pedantic behavior, but he took no notice, and continued to make his boys wash the trunks day after day. It is said in historical documents that he was "obsessed with cleanliness as a habit."

## 张飞酒醉失徐州

《三国演义》中第十四回中的故事。刘备离徐州兵伐袁术，张飞请求守城。刘备说："你酒后刚强，鞭挞士卒，守不得此城。"张飞说："弟从今以后，不饮酒，不打军士。"刘备离城后，张飞宴请守城各官赴席，说今日酒醉，明日戒酒守城，并向众官把盏。有一名叫曹豹的军官，不会饮酒，被张飞鞭打五十。当夜，曹豹写信给吕布，叫他速来夺城。四更天，吕布带兵来徐州，曹豹开城。张飞酒醉未醒，十八骑保着张飞杀出东门，去见刘备。图为张飞向刘备请罪情景。

## ZHANG FEI GETS DRUNK AND LOSES JINGZHOU

This is a story from The Three Kingdoms. Liu Bei left Xuzhou to suppress Yuan Shu. Zhang Fei pleaded to be allowed to guard the city. Liu Bei said: "You cannot protect the city because you lose your judgment after drinking and start beating the soldiers." "I will neither drink nor beat the men from now on," Zhang Fei vowed. After Liu Bei set out, Zhang Fei held a banquet for the various officials, and declared that everyone should drink their fill that day as wine was forbidden the following day. So saying, he rose and began to toast the guests. One officer named Cao Bao could not drink wine and was given fifty lashes by Zhang Fei as punishment. That night Cao Bao wrote a letter to Lü Bu telling him to reoccupy the city as soon as possible. Just before dawn, Lü Bu took his troops to Xuzhou. Cao Bao opened the city gate and let the enemy surge into the city. Zhang Fei was still drunk, and guarded by eighteen cavalry commanders, escaped through the eastern gate to go to Liu Bei. This painting shows Zhang Fei apologizing for his errors to Liu Bei.

## 两县令竞义婚孤女

《醒世恒言》中故事。宋朝，有个叫贾昌的小商人被诬告，定了死罪。多亏新来的石县令，查清冤情，无罪释放了他。这一年，天火烧光了县里粮仓，石县令定为死罪，家产充公，女儿被拍卖。贾昌托人赎出了石县令独生女儿月香，视如亲生。贾昌老婆心地不好，嫌弃月香，趁贾昌经商在外，将月香卖给了县令钟离义作女儿的陪嫁丫鬟。月香又回到了县衙，想起爸爸，哭了起来。钟县令知道月香遭遇后，认月香为干女儿，并将亲女和干女同时嫁给高县令的两个儿子。

## TWO COUNTY MAGISTRATES WITH A POOR GIRL

This is a story from Xingshihengyan. In the Song Dynasty (420-479) lived a trader named Jia Chang. He was framed for a crime and sentenced to death. Fortunately a new county magistrate named Shi took up office at that time. He learned the facts of this injustice and set the trader free. That year a raging fire burned down the county granary, and the county magistrate Shi was sentenced to death. All his properties were confiscated and his daughter was sold. Jia Chang solicited help and redeemed the magistrate's daughter Yuexiang. He treated her like his own daughter. Jia Chang's wife was not very kindhearted. She disliked Yuexiang and sold her to county magistrate Zhong Liyi as his daughter's maid and to serve as part of her dowry while Jia Chang was away on business. Yuexiang therefore once again returned to the county magistrate's residence, her former home. It reminded her of her father and she could not help crying. After county magistrate Zhong learned of Yuexiang's misfortune, he took her as his adopted daughter and married her and his own daughter to county magistrate Gao's two sons.

## 关云长刮骨疗毒

《三国演义》中第七十五回故事。关云长右臂中箭，见箭头有毒，毒已入骨。忽一日，有一人从江东驾小舟而来，自言姓华名陀，因闻关将军乃天下英雄，特来医治。华陀看完云长臂伤，用尖刀割开皮肉，直至入骨，见骨已青。陀用刀刮骨，悉悉有声，帐上帐下将士掩面失色。云长饮酒食肉，谈笑弈棋。华陀刮去骨上箭毒，用药敷之，以线缝之。云长大笑而起道："先生真神医也！"华陀曰："某为医一生，未尝如此。君侯真天神也！"

## SCRAPE THE POISON OFF THE BONE

This is a story from The Three Kingdoms. Guan Yunchang's right arm had been pierced by a poisoned arrow, and ulceration soon reached the bone. One day a man arrived unexpectedly by boat from south of the Yangtze River, saying that he was Hua Tuo. Hearing that General Guan was a world-renowned hero, he had made a special trip to cure him. After examining the wound, Hua Tuo cut through to the bone with a knife and found the bone was already coated green, and scraped the poison off the bone. The knife made a thin, grating sound as it scraped the surface, and everyone present blanched and covered his face. But Guan Yunchang continued eating and drinking, laughing and talking as he played chess. Hua Tuo finished scraping, applied medicine, and sewed the wound shut. Guan Yunchang got up, smiled, and said: "Master, you are a marvelous physician." Hua Tuo replied, "In a lifetime of practice I have never seen anything like this! It is Your Lordship who is more than human!"

## 《陆绩怀橘》

元代王实甫所作。东汉末年，大约公元200年，陆绩6岁的时候，随父到江东富豪袁术家作客。袁术令家人拿鲜橘给他吃。陆绩先拿小的吃了，觉得很甜，又拿了三个大的放在怀里。傍晚，陆绩向主人鞠躬告辞，橘子从陆绩怀里滚出。袁术便问："陆郎，你来我家作客，为什么要拿走橘子呢？"陆绩跪下道："我母亲最爱吃橘子，你的橘子甘甜味美，想拿三个让他尝尝。"袁术听了陆绩回答，连称："孝子！孝子！"陆绩长大后，成了江西九江有名的孝子，并博学多才，能注易、释玄、晓算数。

## LU JI CONCEALS ORANGES IN HIS CLOTHES

At the end of the Eastern Jin Dynasty, around 200 AD, Lu Ji, at the age of six, went with his father to visit Yuan Shu, a rich and powerful man who lived south of the Yangtze River. Yuan Shu asked his men to serve Lu Ji with some oranges. Lu Ji first tried the smallest and found it very sweet, so he snatched three big oranges and hid them inside his clothes. At dusk, when Lu Ji bowed down to say goodbye to the host, the oranges spilled out. Yuan Shu asked: "Little boy, you came to my home as a guest, why do you take oranges away?" Lu Ji knelt down and said: "My mother likes oranges very much. Your oranges are very sweet and flavorful, so I wanted to take three for her." Hearing what Lu Ji had said, Yuan Shu praised him again and again, "A filial son, a filial son indeed." After Lu Ji grew up, he became a well-known filial son in Jiujiang, Jiangxi and also an erudite scholar.

## 《西厢记》

故事发生在唐代，公元785年。书生张生赶考奔赴长安。这一日，来到山西永济县，入普救寺拜菩萨，在寺内巧遇相国之女崔莺莺，心生爱意，不想再谋功名，便在寺内借住。此时，乱贼孙飞虎率兵包围普救寺，要抢崔莺莺为妻。老夫人被迫许诺，谁能退贼，便将莺莺许配与他。张生写信求好友杜确率兵星夜来救，生擒了孙飞虎。老夫人得了救却想赖婚。莺莺在丫鬟红娘的帮助下，在西厢与张生私好。《西厢记》编成各种戏曲，数百年在中国舞台上久演不衰。

## THE WEST CHAMBER

This story took place in 785 during the Tang Dynasty. The scholar Zhang Sheng was on his way to Chang'an to take the imperial examination. One day he arrived at Yongji County, Shanxi and went to pray in the Pujiu Temple, where he ran into Cui Yingying, the daughter of the prime minister. He fell in love with her at first sight and did not want to go to the capital to seek a career. He decided to stay at the temple for a while. One day, Sun Feihu, a bandit chieftain, took his men and surrounded the temple. He wanted to snatch Cui Yingying away and make her his wife. Cui's mother had no idea of any such plan, but was forced to promise that she would marry her daughter to whoever could repel the bandits. Zhang Sheng wrote a letter to his friend Du Que who later came with his troops and captured Sun Feihu. Cui's mother and her daughter were saved, but Cui's mother broke her promise. With the help of Hong Niang, Cui Yingying's maid, Cui Yingying and Zhang Sheng came together in the West Chamber. The West Chamber has been employed into various dramas and has been popular on the Chinese stage for hundreds of years.

## 天女散花

佛经故事。如来佛有一名叫维摩洁的弟子（Vimalakirti）经常托病在家一人悟佛。如来佛派弟子们前去看望，他便借此向来人讲经说法。一日，如来佛正在莲花座上讲演佛法，忽见一片瑞云从东边飘来，便知弟子维摩洁又在＂患病＂，于是派诸菩萨和众弟子前去问候。天女身着彩衣，手提花篮，也来到人间，见维摩洁正在讲法，众弟子在听，便将满篮鲜花倾底散去。鲜花在每个菩萨身上脱落，惟在舍利弗的身上沾满不脱。维摩洁说：＂结习未尽，鲜花着身；结习尽者，鲜花不着。＂舍利弗听后，决心加倍修行。

## CELESTIAL MAIDS SCATTER FLOWERS

This is a story from Buddhist Scriptures. Buddha Tathagata had a disciple named Vimalakirti, who often pleaded illness and practiced Buddhism at home alone. When Tathagata sent his disciples to see him, he would use this opportunity to preach the dharma to visitors. One day, when Buddha Tathagata was lecturing on Buddhist doctrine, he suddenly saw a crowd of clouds floating up from the east and knew that his disciple Vimalakirti was "sick" again. He then sent deities and disciples to see him. Celestial maids in colorful clothes holding flower baskets also came to earth. They saw that Vimalakirti was preaching and his disciples were listening, and raised their flower baskets, letting the flowers drift down. The flowers slipped off the bodies of all deities except Sariputra whose body was covered with flowers. Vimalakirti said: "Flowers stick to those who have not realized the Way but do not stay on those who have achieved it." Hearing this, Sariputra determined to double his efforts in practicing Buddhism.

## 博望坡诸葛亮初用兵

刘备自得诸葛亮，以师礼待之。关、张二人不悦说："诸葛亮年幼，有甚才学！兄长待之太过。"刘备答："吾得他，犹鱼之得水也。"忽报曹操差夏侯惇引兵十万，杀奔新野来了。刘备和关、张商议抗敌，张飞便对刘备说："哥哥何不使'水'去挡曹兵。"刘备说："智在军师，勇须二弟。"诸葛亮恐关、张不肯听号令。便从刘备手里接过剑印。诸葛亮这才调三千兵马，在博望坡，采用火攻，杀退曹兵十万。这是《三国演义》中第三十九回故事。

## ZHUGE LIANG MAKES HIS DEBUT AT BOWANGPO

This is a story from Chapter Thirty-Nine of The Three Kingdoms. Ever since Liu Bei had appointed Zhuge Liang as his military adviser, he had treated him with due respect. Guan Yunchang and Zhang Fei said unhappily, "Zhuge Liang is so young. What knowledge or ability could he have? Haven't you treated him too well?" Liu Bei answered: "He is to me as water to fish." Suddenly they were informed that Cao Cao had sent Xia Houdun with 100,000 soldiers to Xinye. Liu Bei discussed methods of resisting the enemy with Guan Yunchang and Zhang Fei. Zhang Fei said to Liu Bei, "Brother, why don't you use 'water' to resist the Cao's army?" Liu Bei said: "For brains, I have Zhuge Liang; for courage, I have you two." Zhuge Liang was afraid that Guan and Zhang would not obey his orders, so he took over the sword and seal from Liu Bei, and dispatched 3,000 armed forces to attack the enemies using fire at Bowangpo, defeating Cao Cao's 100,000 troops.

## 天仙配

故事发生在古代。王母娘娘的七个美丽的外孙女在天宫里整日织锦，深感寂寞，便来人间游玩，遇上地上孝子董永卖身葬父，去傅员外家上工。七仙女可怜董永身世，又爱他忠厚老实，请老槐树为媒，土地神主婚，与董永结成夫妻。后来，玉皇大帝得知七仙女下凡，派天兵天将下界，令七仙女午时三刻返回天廷，否则杀死董永。天仙配故事编成黄梅戏，又排成电影。因为其唱腔优美，所以中国老百姓都会唱上二句。

## A CELESTIAL MARRIAGE

This story took place in the Han Dynasty (206BC - AD25). The seven beautiful granddaughters of the Queen Mother of the West felt so bored with brocade weaving all day long in the Heavenly Palace that they descended to earth to have some fun. They ran into Dong Yong on his way to work at the official Fu's home. Dong Yong's father died, but Dong Yong had no money to bury his father. As a filial son, he sold himself to the Fu family for money to bury his father. The seventh girl showed her sympathy for Dong Yong's life and fell in love with this kind and honest man. She asked an old Chinese scholar tree to be her matchmaker and the God of Earth to hold the wedding ceremony, and married Dong Yong. Later the Jade Emperor learned that the seventh grand daughter had descended to earth and sent heavenly troops to catch her. He ordered her to return to heaven at 3pm, otherwise he would kill Dong Yong. This story has been made into Huangmei Drama (a regional drama in Anhui) and a film. As the drama has some sweet tunes, most Chinese people can sing a few of its songs.

## 《示金陵子》

李白（701～762年）一生写下900余首脍炙人口的诗篇。当李白61岁时，子身一人来到金陵游玩。夜晚，他凭窗观赏金陵秋色，不由得抚琴作歌。歌声引来一名年轻美貌的歌女，愿陪伴李白。李白兴致勃勃，携同少女，迎着秋日落花，渡江西去。李白想，能与这一美女在林泉之中同行，实为一大快事！《示金陵子》全诗如下：

> "金陵城东谁家子，窃听琴声碧窗里。
> 落花一片天上来，随人直渡西江水。
> 楚歌吴语娇不成，似能未能最有情。
> 谢公正要东山妓，携手林泉处处行。"

## A GIRL IN JINLING

Li Bai (701-762) wrote more than nine hundred popular poems in his life. At the age of sixty-one Li Bai went alone to visit Jinling (present Nanjing). One night, as he looked out of the window and enjoyed the autumn scenery of Jinling he was so happy he could not help but play the pipa while composing songs. A pretty singsong girl was attracted by his songs and willing to keep him company. Li Bai was delighted. He went across the river to the west with the girl, facing the fallen flowers of autumn. He thought what a joyful thing in life it was to be able to travel with such a pretty girl in the forest and waters. The poem he wrote says:

> "Which family is this girl from at the eastern city of Jinling,
> Listening to the zither stealthily inside the window.
> Flower petals fell from the sky,
> Following us across the river to the west.
> The Chu songs and Wu words are not mild enough,
> Love is expressed the best through likelihood and impossibility
> Thank God for sending me an eastern hill singsong girl,
> To travel around in the forest and waters with, hand in hand.

## 封三娘

《聊斋志异》中故事。元宵节这天，范十一娘到水月寺看众尼作法会，结识一位绝代佳人封三娘。归家后，十一娘想念三娘，怅然得病。重阳节这天，十一娘在园中见一女子攀墙窥望，正是封三娘。从此，封三娘成为十一娘闺中良友。春日郊游，见秀才孟安仁，布袍不饰容仪俊伟。三娘替十一娘私订婚约。有一权贵为子向范家求婚，范公畏之，应下婚事。迎亲那天，十一娘上吊自尽。孟安仁到十一娘坟上哭泣。封三娘让挖墓破棺，背十一娘回家，用药灌之，十一娘复活，与孟安仁结为夫妻。封三娘告诉他们，她是狐仙。第二年，孟安仁中状元、进翰林。那权贵父子因犯国法被发配充军去了。

## FENG SANNIANG

This is a story from Strange Tales from the Make-Do Studio. On the day of the Lantern Festival Lady Fan Shiyi went to the Water and Moon Monastery to see the Buddhist ceremony held by nuns, where she met the beautiful lady Feng Sanniang. After returning home, Lady Fan missed Sanniang so much that she fell ill. On the ninth day of the ninth month of the lunar calendar, the Double Ninth Festival, Lady Fan saw a girl looking at her from the top of the outside wall. It was Feng Sanniang. From then on, Feng became Lady Fan's intimate friend. One day on a spring outing, Feng ran into Meng Anren, a young and handsome scholar, dressed in plain clothes, and helped Lady Fan arrange a secret marriage with him. A few days later, an influential official proposed his son in marriage to the Fan family. Lady Fan's father was afraid of his power and forced to agree. On the wedding day Lady Fan committed suicide by hanging herself. The scholar Meng Anren went to her tomb and wept for her. Feng let him dig up the tomb, carry her body home, and pour some medicine into her mouth. Following her instructions, Lady Fan revived and married Meng Anren. Feng then told them that she was a fox spirit. The next year, Meng Anren won first place in the imperial examinations and became a member of the Imperial Academy. The influential official and his son were sent to a remote outpost to do hard labor for an offence against the national law.

## 孔融让梨

孔融是孔子（前551～前479年）第二十代世孙。孔融四岁的时候，父亲从外面买回一些梨，让孩子们分着吃。哥哥姐姐让孔融先拿，他选个最小的。父亲问他为什么，他说："我年纪最小，应该吃小梨。"孔融礼让的孩童美德，千百年来一直在中国传颂。古时，又把这个故事编入起蒙课本《三字经》。汉献帝时(190-220)，孔融为北海太守八年，敬老爱幼，甚得民心。

## KONG RONG OFFERS A PEAR TO OTHERS

Kong Rong was the twentieth descendant son of Confucius (551-478BC). When Kong Rong was aged four, his father bought some pears home one day for his children to eat. Kong Rong's brothers and sisters made him choose first. Kong Rong selected the smallest one. When his father asked him the reason, he said: "I'm the youngest in the family. I should have the smallest pear." The story of Kong Rong's modesty when offering pears has passed on from generation to generation in China for thousands of years. It was also edited into the enlightenment textbook The Three Character Primer. Kong Rong worked as the grand protector of Beihai for six years during the reign of Emperor Xian of the Han Dynasty (190-220). He respected the elderly and loved the young and enjoyed the immense popular support of the people.

## 林黛玉焚稿断痴情

《红楼梦》中第九十七回故事。黛玉知道宝玉和宝钗的婚事后，口吐鲜血，气息微细，病日重一日，自料万无生理，让丫鬟雪雁开箱，要那块宝玉送她的旧手帕，她在上面题有对宝玉深情的诗句。又让雪雁笼上火盆，挪到身边，瞅着那火点点头，将手帕往上一撂，回手又把那诗稿拿起来，撂在火上，把眼一闭，往后一仰，不省人事。就在宝玉和宝钗成亲那天晚上，黛玉直声叫道："宝玉，宝玉，你好……"便浑身冷汗，两眼一翻，香魂一缕随风散，气绝身亡。

## LIN DAIYU BURNS HER POEMS TO END HER INFATUATION

This is a story from Chapter Ninety-Seven of A Dream of Red Mansions. After learning of the marriage of Baoyu and Baochai, Lin Daiyu vomited blood and breathed faintly. Her illness became severer day by day. She knew that her days were numbered and asked her maid Xueyan to open her case and fetch the old handkerchief given to her by Baoyu, on which she had written some verses. She then ordered Xueyan to light the brazier and put it at her side. She looked at the fire and nodded, then dropped the handkerchief on it. She turned and picked up her poems and put them on fire too. She closed her eyes, sank back and lost consciousness. On the evening of the wedding of Baoyu and Baochai, Daiyu cried: "Baoyu, Baoyu! How...." She broke out in a cold sweat and died in a second with eyes turned up. Her sweet soul was gone with the wind.

## 尧王访舜

国君尧穿粗布衣，吃糙米，为君一百年，为民做了无数好事。尧老了，要把王位传给天下贤人，而不传给儿子丹米，因为他只知吃喝玩乐。有个叫舜的青年，孤身一人在历山开荒种地，那里农民受到舜的感化，愿把好地让给别人耕种；舜去打鱼，又感化渔民相让好的渔场；舜去做陶器，影响陶工做精美耐用的陶器。舜走到哪里，哪里的居民增加。尧就把王位让给舜，又把两个女儿娥皇、女英嫁给舜为妻。舜做了国君，舜老了以后，知道儿子商均只知唱歌跳舞，又把王位传给为民治水的禹。

## KING YAO VISITS SHUN

In the 26th to 21st century BC, King Yao wore coarse cloth and ate coarse food grains. He had been king for a hundred years and did a lot of good for the people. In his old age he wanted to pass his throne on to a wise man of the world instead of his son Danmi, who only enjoyed eating, drinking, playing and having fun. There was a young man named Shun. He lived alone and exploited the virgin land. Under his influence, the farmers there all gave their good land to others to farm. When Shun went fishing, he made fishers realize that they should give the best fishing ground to others. When Shun went to make pottery, he convinced the potters to make refined and durable pottery. No matter where Shun went, the population increased. At last, King Yao passed his throne on to Shun and married his two daughters Erhuang and Nuying to him. Shun knew that his son Shang Jun was only interested in singing and dancing, and so in his old age he abdicated in favor of Yu who tamed rivers for the good of the people.

## 八卦炉中逃大圣

孙悟空被玉帝封为齐天大圣，在天宫偷吃仙桃、仙酒、仙丹，返回花果山被捉，绑在降妖柱上，被刀砍斧剁，枪刺剑刽，莫想伤及其身。太上老君向玉帝奏道："我那五壶丹，被他吃在肚里，所以浑做金钢之躯，急不能伤。不若道领去，放在八卦炉中，以文武火煅炼。炼出我的丹来，他身为灰烬矣。"大圣被推入八卦炉中，钻进风眼。不觉四十九天，老君的火候俱全。忽一日，开炉取丹。大圣将身一纵，跳出丹炉，蹬倒八卦炉，往外就走。这是《西游记》中第七回故事。

THE STORIES BEHIND THE LONG CORRIDOR PAINTINGS AT THE SUMMER PALACE

## THE GREAT SAGE ESCAPES FROM THE EIGHT TRIGRAMS FURNACE

This is a story from Chapter Seven of Journey to the West. After Sun Wukong was conferred the title Great Sage Equaling Heaven by the Jade Emperor, he stole peaches of immortality, drank the imperial liquor, ate the elixir pills in heaven and returned to the Flowers and Fruit Mountain. He was then captured and tied to the Demon-subduing Pillar. They hacked at him with sabers, sliced at him with axes, lunged at him with spears and cut at him with swords, but they were unable to inflict a single wound on him. The Lord Lao Zi reported to the Jade Emperor, "My five gourds of elixir pills were swallowed by him, so his body has become a diamond that cannot be harmed. Let me take him and put him in my Eight Trigrams Furnace, where I can refine out my elixir with civil and martial fire and reduce him to ashes at the same time." The Great Sage was pushed into the Eight Trigrams Furnace. He squeezed himself into the "Palace of Sun." Forty-nine days had passed and Lord Lao Zi's fire had reached the required temperature and burned for long enough. Finally, the furnace was opened so as to extract the elixir. The Great Sage leapt out of the furnace, kicked it over with a crash, and took off.

## 穆桂英飞索套宗保

《杨家将》中故事。宗保押粮草途经穆柯寨，见父亲手下大将孟良被穆桂英战败，催马挺枪上前，大战穆桂英五十余回合，两人不分胜负。穆桂英见宗保少年英俊，武艺高强，有心以身相许，佯装不敌宗保败走，宗保紧追不舍，穆桂英回身抛出红罗套，套住宗保，从马上活捉。这是穆桂英招亲中一段故事。

## MU GUIYING CAPTURES YANG ZONGBAO

This is a story from The Generals of the Yang Family. Yang Zongbao was escorting a transport of army provisions through Mount Muke. Seeing Meng Liang, a general of his father's, had been defeated by Mu Guiying, he raced his horse forward and with his lance and fought 50 rounds without any result. Overcome by Yang Zongbao's handsome looks and outstanding martial skills, Mu Guiying wanted to marry him. She retreated in feigned defeat and made Yang Zongbao chase after her. Mu Guiying then turned, threw out a red net and caught Yang Zongbao. This is a part from the story of Mu Guiying taking Yang Zongbao as her husband.

## 三英战吕布

《三国演义》中第五回故事。东汉末年，全国十八路诸侯推袁绍为盟主，兵马奔洛阳，连营三百里，讨伐董贼。董卓起兵二十万，亲率十五万守住离洛阳五十里的虎牢关。董卓义子吕布率兵五万在关前扎住大寨。袁绍派八路诸侯攻打。吕布出战，接连杀伤几

## THREE HEROES FIGHT WITH LÜ BU

This is a story from Chapter Five of The Three Kingdoms. At the end of the Eastern Han Dynasty in 190, Yuan Shao, elected as leader of the union by the eighteen lords of the realm, led a punitive expedition to Dong Zhuo in Luoyang, and pitched camp over an area of 150 kilometers. Dong Zhuo sent two hundred thousand troops against the lords and he himself led 150,000 troops to guard Tiger Trap Pass, located some 25 kilometers from Luoyang. Dong Zhuo's adopted son Lü Bu took 50,000 troops to guard the front of the pass. Yuan Shao ordered eight lords to attack. Lü Bu

员大将，八路诸侯齐出，都不是吕布对手。正在危急，张飞杀出，大战吕布五十余回合，不分胜负。关云长见了，把马一拍，舞八十二斤青龙偃月刀，来夹攻吕布，又战三十合，战不倒吕布。刘备掣双股剑，刺斜里也来助战。这就是虎牢关三英战吕布。

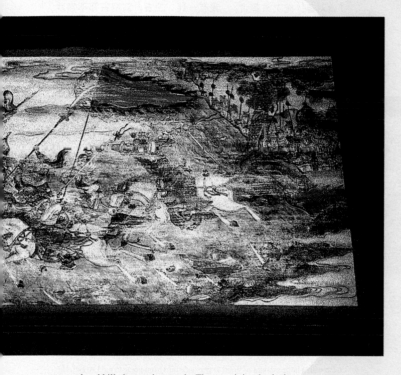

emerged and killed several generals. The remaining lords then mounted their horses and fought with Lü Bu, but no one could match him. At this moment, Zhang Fei flew at Lü Bu and fought more than 50 rounds. Seeing that neither could best the other, Guan Yunchang urged his horse forward and, flourishing his crescent-moon blade, attacked Lü Bu from another side. They fought another thirty rounds, but Lü Bu was unconquerable. Liu Bei, clenching his matching swords, angled his way onto the field to help. This is the story of three heroes fighting with Lü Bu at the Tiger Trap Pass.

## 吕布辕门射戟

《三国演义》中第十六回故事。南阳太守袁术见刘备军屯小沛，
容易攻取，要先伐刘备。奈吕布虎踞徐州，便先送二十万斛粟米，
让吕布按兵不动。遣纪灵为大将，统兵十万，进攻小沛。吕布懂
得唇亡齿寒的道理，引兵来沛县一里扎下营寨。纪灵责吕布无信。
布请刘备、纪灵来寨说："我有一计，使袁、刘两家都不怨我，
尽在天命。"令左右接过画戟，去辕门外远远插定，回顾纪灵、
刘备说："吾若一箭射中戟小枝，你两家罢兵；如射不中，你们
安排厮杀。"吕布箭射画戟，才引出后人诗："雕羽翎飞箭到时，
雄兵十万脱征衣。"

## LÜ BU DEMONSTRATES HIS MARKSMANSHIP BEFORE HIS CAMP

This is a story from Chapter Sixteen of The Three Kingdoms. Seeing Liu Bei
stationed in Xiaopei, which was very easy to take, Yuan Shu wanted first to suppress
Liu Bei, but he was afraid of Lü Bu who controlled Xuzhou. He therefore presented
Lü Bu with a large amount of grain to persuade him from going to aid Liu Bei. He
then commanded Ji Ling to lead tens of thousands of troops against Xiaopei. Lü Bu
knew pretty well that if Yuan Shu overcame Liu Bei, he would be in danger, so he
led a force to a place 500 meters away from Xiaopei. Ji Ling accused Lü Bu of bad
faith, and Lü Bu invited Liu Bei and Ji Ling to his camp saying to them, "I think I
have a way to satisfy both sides. It is in Heaven's hands." Lü Bu handed his weapon
to his attendants and had it planted in the ground, well in front of the entrance to his
camp. Then, turning to his guests, he said, "If I hit the small side blade with one shot,
you will call off your war. If I miss, you are free to return to your camps and prepare
for battle." Lü Bu's perfect hit made later generations write poetry in praise of him:
"The leopard-tail quivered on the halberd haft, one hundred thousand men untied
their gear."

## 斩蔡阳兄弟释疑

《三国演义》中第二十八回故事。关云长过五关斩六将，保刘备二夫人向汝南进发，路经古城，得知张飞在这里，命人入城通报。张飞听罢，随即披挂持矛上马出城，见关云长挥矛便搠。关云长大惊，便叫："贤弟何故如此？"张飞认为忠臣宁死不辱。大丈夫岂有事二主之理？必是曹操派关云长来捉自己。云长说："我若捉你，须带军马来。"张飞把手指曰："兀的不是军马来也！"须臾，曹军至。为首一将乃是蔡阳。关云长不打话，举刀便砍，刀起处，蔡阳头已落地。张飞遂请二嫂入城。二夫人诉说关云长历过之事，张飞方才大哭，参拜云长。

## SLAYING CAI YANG TO DISPEL HIS BROTHERS' DOUBTS

This is a story from Chapter Twenty-Eight of The Three Kingdoms. After Guan Yunchang had slain six generals and breached five passes, he escorted Liu Bei's two ladies on to Runan. When he passed the city of Gucheng, he learned that Zhang Fei was there and asked that his presence be reported to him. Having heard that Guan Yunchang had arrived, Zhang Fei armed himself, mounted his horse and went out of the city. He brandished his spear at Guan Yunchang. With great astonishment Guan Yunchang shouted, "What does this mean, worthy brother?" Zhang Fei thought that a loyal vassal prefers death to disgrace. What self-respecting man served two masters? It must have been Cao Cao who sent Guan Yunchang here to catch him. Guan Yunchang said, "Wouldn't I need an army if I were here to capture you?" Zhang Fei cried, "What's that?" pointing at the troops. In an instant, Cao Cao's troops came led by Cai Yang. Guan Yunchang said nothing. He lifted his blade and chopped Cai Yang's head off. Zhang Fei led the two ladies into the city. After hearing the ladies' description of the events, Zhang Fei wept and bowed deeply to Guan Yunchang.

## 唐僧夜阻通天河

《西游记》中第四十七回故事。唐僧师徒四人晓行夜住，渴饮饥餐。一日月夜，来到通天河边，见河碑题字："河宽八百里，亘古少人行。"他们在陈家庄陈老员外家投住，得知通天河里有一灵感大王，每年要吃一对童男童女，今年轮到陈家。悟空和八戒变成陈家童男童女，把妖精打下通天河。

## THE TANG PRIEST IS STOPPED BY THE RIVER OF HEAVEN AT NIGHT

This is a story from Chapter Forty-Seven of Journey to the West. The Tang Priest and his disciples were traveling to the West for Buddhist scriptures. One night, they reached the bank of the River of Heaven and saw a stone tablet on which was inscribed "Four hundred kilometers across, few travelers have ever been here." They came to an old official, Chen's home to beg for a night's shelter. The old man told them that in the river was a Great King of Miraculous Response, who ate a boy and a girl every year. This year it was Chen's turn to offer his son and daughter to the king. Sun Wukong and Pig turned into Chen's boy and girl and beat the evil spirit down to the River of

那灵感大王用计作法，起寒风，降大雪，把通天河冻结。
师徒四人在通天河冰上赶路。正走着，妖怪在河底迸开
冰冻，将唐僧捉了去。悟空请来观世音菩萨降了妖怪。
原来那怪是莲花池里金鱼，每日浮头听经，修成手段。
悟空让陈家庄人来拜活观音，内有善图画者，画下鱼篮
观音神影，流传至今。

Heaven. The Great King of Miraculous Response then used his
powers to call up wind, bring snow, and freeze the rivers. Seeing
the river had been frozen, the Tang Priest and his disciples
quickly set out. As they walked, the evil spirit made the ice burst
open from the bottom of the river and took the Tang Priest away.
Sun Wukong went to ask the Bodhisattva for help, and eventually
the evil spirit was suppressed by the Bodhisattva. It was
originally a goldfish in a lotus pond that swam up to listen to
sutras every day and trained itself in magic powers. Sun Wukong
finally let the people in Chen Village see the living Bodhisattva.
Among the villagers was a good painter who left to posterity a
painting of the Bodhisattva appearing with a fish-basket, which
was passed on for generations.

## 刘备跃马过檀溪

刘备投荆州刘表。一日，刘表邀刘备饮酒时，潸然泪下。原来刘表有两子，前妻陈氏生刘琦，后妻蔡氏生刘琮。表欲立长子，奈蔡氏族中皆掌军务。刘备说："自古废长立幼必乱。若蔡氏权重，可徐徐削之。"蔡氏偷听，心甚恨之。蔡氏与兄弟蔡瑁利用刘表宴请抚慰九郡四十二州官员之机，欲除刘

## LIU BEI VAULTS THE TANXI RIVER ON HORSEBACK

Liu Bei went to Liu Biao in Jingzhou for shelter. One day, Liu Biao invited Liu Bei to a banquet, at which he suddenly began to weep. Liu Biao told Liu Bei that he had two sons, Liu Qi from his previous wife Chen, and Liu Zong from his present wife Cai. He wanted to leave the elder son as his heir, but he was afraid of the Cai clan because they controlled the military power. Liu Bei said: "Since the most ancient times, removing the elder and confirming the younger has led to disaster. If you are worried about the extent of the Cai clan's power, try paring it down a little at a time." Lady Cai heard this from behind a screen and bitterly resented what Liu Bei had said. She asked her

备。酒至三巡，有人暗示刘备此事。刘备借口方便，开
后园门，飞身上马出西门而走。行无数里，前有檀溪数
丈宽，后有追兵。刘备着慌，纵马下溪，马的前蹄忽陷，
刘备加鞭大呼，那马从水中跃身而起，一跳三丈，飞上
西岸。这是《三国演义》中第三十四回故事。

brother Cai Mao to eliminate Liu Bei at the commanders'
banquet. During the third round of wine Liu Bei took the advice
of an informant and went at once to the privy. He opened the gate
of the back courtyard, vaulted into the saddle and fled by the
western gate. Liu Bei had traveled for only a short distance when
he was stopped by the Tanxi River, several rods broad. Seeing the
pursuers were catching up, Liu Bei, at his wit's end, charged into
the racing current. After a few paces the horse lost its footing.
Belaboring the horse, he shouted, "A jinxed horse, indeed! Today
you have brought me misfortune." But the horse reared and,
making thirty spans with every thrust, gained the opposite shore.

## 玉堂春

故事发生在公元1506-1521年，明代。礼部尚书之子王金龙携带数万两白银，进北京读书，遇名妓玉堂春，愿结百年之好。两人山盟海誓。王金龙在妓院住了一年光景，囊空如洗，被老鸨赶了出来，沦为街头乞丐，夜宿破庙之中。玉堂春不忘王公子情意，四处打听他的下落，倾囊相助自己的积蓄和首饰，劝他回家读书，早日取得功名。从此，玉堂春拒绝别的客人。老鸨子将她卖给山西富商沈燕林。那富商妻子皮氏早与人私通，毒死亲夫反诬诿玉堂春所为，她买通县官。县令严刑逼供，定玉堂春死罪。王金龙连科及第，做了八府巡按，查出玉堂春冤情，两人正式结为夫妻。中国京剧《苏三起解》，人人皆知。

## YU TANGCHUN

This story took place during the years 1506-1521 of the Ming Dynasty. Wang Jinlong, the son of the minister of rites, went to study in the capital, today's Beijing, taking with him thousands of pieces of silver. He met a courtesan Yu Tangchun and decided to marry her. The two made a solemn pledge of love for each other. Wang Jinlong lived at the brothel for a year, spent all his money, and was eventually driven out by the brothel owner. He begged in the streets during the day and stayed overnight at a shabby temple. Yu Tangchun could not forget Wang and looked for him everywhere. She sold all her jewelry and used her life savings to persuade him to return home and continue studying for his future career. From then on, she refused to see other guests. The owner of the brothel sold her to Shen Yanlin, a rich merchant in Shanxi. The man's wife Lady Pi had a love affair with another man. She poisoned her husband and bribed the county magistrate into framing Yu Tangchun for the murder. The county magistrate used cruel torture to force Yu Tangchun to confess, and then sentenced her to death. Wang Jinlong passed the imperial examination and was promoted to governor of eight prefectures. While looking through the court cases he noticed that an injustice had been perpetrated against Yu Tangchun, and heard the case again. The two married in the end. This story was made into a popular Beijing Opera piece.

## 王佐断臂

《说岳全传》中的故事。公元1127～1131年，南宋高宗年间，金国屡犯中原。岳家军与金兀术在朱仙镇交锋。金国小将陆文龙，手持双枪出战，岳家将无一人能敌。岳飞坐在帐中，苦思破敌无策。统制官王佐，自断一条臂，满身是血，要诈降金营，伺机刺杀金兀术，使岳飞感动。王佐来金营，金兀

## WANG ZUO CUTS OFF HIS ARM

This is a story from the Biography of Yue Fei. In the reign of Emperor Gao Zong (1127-1131) of the Southern Song Dynasty, the State of Jin frequently invaded the Central Plains. Yue Fei's army engaged in a battle with Jin Wuzhu at Zhuxian Town. Lu Wenlong, a young general of the State of Jin, emerged armed with a sword in each hand. Nobody from Yue army could match him. Yue Fei sat in his tent pondering a way to deal with him. Wang Zuo, a general in Yue's army, cut off one of his arms as a means to fake defection, and waited for the chance to kill Jin Wuzhu in the Jin camp. Yue Fei was deeply moved by Wang's courage. Wang Zuo came to the Jin camp to

术不疑，留在帐前。王佐接近陆文龙的奶娘张氏，得知陆文龙乃宋臣潞安州节度使陆登的儿子。16年前，金兵破城，陆登夫妇遇难。金兀术抱回才出生几个月的陆文龙，收为义子。一日，王佐来陆文龙帐内说书，讲出陆文龙的身世，使陆文龙归宋抗金。王佐断臂的故事广为流传，还有年画张贴。

surrender and won the trust of Jin Wuzhu, who kept him by his side to serve as a guard. On meeting Lady Zhang, Lu Wenlong's wet nurse, Wang Zuo learned that Lu Wenlong was actually the son of Lu Deng, a Song general who had died at his post resisting the Jin army. Lu Wenlong, then only months old, had been taken away by Jin Wuzhu and raised as his adopted son. One day, Wang Zuo went to Lu Wenlong's tent to tell stories. He took this chance to tell Lu how his family had been murdered by the Jin army and persuaded him to join the Song to fight the Jin army. This story was also made into a New Year's Painting to paste on household walls.

## 得金珠吕布忘义杀丁原

董卓进京后，大排筵宴，遍请公乡。酒行数巡，厉声曰："吾欲
废帝，立陈留王。"百官不敢出声。荆州刺史丁原大呼："不可，
不可！"卓大怒，欲杀丁原，见丁原背后一人，手执方天画戟，
乃丁原义子吕布也。次日，丁原引军城外搦战，董卓引军出迎，
吕布飞马直杀过来，董卓大败。董卓手下中郎将李肃是吕布同乡，
带"赤兔"千里马、黄金一千两、明珠数十颗、玉带一条，来说
吕布降卓。二更天，吕布杀了丁原，拜董卓为义父。这是《三国
演义》中第三回故事。

## AFTER GETTING GOLD AND PEARLS, LÜ BU KILLS DING YUAN

This is a story from Chapter Three of The Three Kingdoms. After Dong Zhuo
entered the capital city, he held a great banquet to which he invited the elder lords
and nobles. After several rounds of wine he shouted, "I shall depose the Emperor
and enthrone the prince." Nobody said a word except Ding Yuan, imperial inspector
of Jingzhou, who shouted, "This is wrong, wrong!" Dong Zhuo became angry and
threatened Ding Yuan, and at this moment spotted a man standing behind him. He
was Lü Bu, Ding Yuan's adopted son, clenching a figured halberd with a two-sided
blade. The next day, Ding Yuan was outside the city with his men spoiling for a
fight, and Dong Zhuo led his forces out to meet them. Lü Bu charged Dong Zhuo
directly and drove Dong Zhuo's army back. Li Su, who worked for Dong Zhuo and
came from the same village as Lü Bu, took the Red Hare horse of extraordinary
speed and stamina, one thousand taels of gold, several dozen lustrous pearls, and a
jade belt to Lü Bu's camp and persuaded him to join Dong Zhuo. Late that night at
the second watch, Lü Bu killed Ding Yuan and honored Dong Zhuo as his foster
father.

## 铡美案

前面谈过秦香莲的故事。北宋时，陈士美中状元，招为驸马，忘记了结发妻子秦香莲和所生儿女，进而还要杀妻灭子。香莲告到开封府，府尹包拯劝陈士美认下香莲母子，否则开封府铁面无私决不轻饶。陈士美认为自己是当朝驸马，蔑视公堂。包拯要铡陈士美，皇姑、国太赶来，包拯摘下乌纱帽，令剑子手抬出虎头铡，行刑！

## EXECUTION OF CHEN SHIMEI

During the Song Dynasty, Chen Shimei won first place in the imperial examinations and married the emperor's daughter, even though he already had a wife, Qin Xianglian and children, whom he wanted dead. Qin Xianglian went to the Court of Kaifeng to sue him. Lord Bao Zhen urged Chen to acknowledge them, otherwise he, as an impartial and incorruptible official, would be forced to prosecute him. As the emperor's son-in-law, Chen regarded himself as above the court, and refused. Lord Bao therefore decided to execute Chen Shimei. In the presence of the emperor's mother and aunt, Lord Bao took off his headwear and ordered the executioner to bring the Tiger Head Cutter to execute Chen on the spot.

## 报兄仇张飞遇害

公元169年，刘、关、张桃园三结义，不求同日生，但求同日死。
公元221年，刘备在蜀中称帝。关云长失荆州遇害。张飞闻知，
旦夕号泣，血湿衣襟，每日望南切齿睁目怒恨。得刘备兵伐东吴
旨意，下令三日内，制白旗白甲，全军挂孝伐吴。帐下两员末将

## EAGER FOR REVENGE, ZHANG FEI IS ASSASSINATED

This is a story from The Three Kingdoms. In 169, Liu Bei, Guan
Yunchang and Zhang Fei pledged mutual faith in a peach garden. They
swore that as they dared not hope to have been born the same day, that
they would die the same day. In 221, Liu Bei proclaimed himself the
emperor of Shu, and Guan Yunchang lost Jingzhou and was killed. When
Zhang Fei learned Guan Yunchang was dead, he howled and wept until
his shirt was damp with tears. Each day he gazed southward, gnashing his
teeth in fury and humiliation, crying out in anguish. When he received Liu
Bei's order to suppress Wu, he ordered white banners and white armor to

范疆、张达入帐说："白旗白甲，一时无措。"飞大怒，叱武士缚二
将于树上，各鞭背五十。并说："若违了限，即杀汝二人示众！"张
达对范疆说："比如他杀我，不如我杀他。我两个若不当死，则他醉
在床上。"当晚，飞令人将酒来与部将同饮，不觉大醉，卧于帐中。
初更时分，二贼密入帐中，以短刀刺入飞腹，飞大叫一声而死。时
年五十五岁。

be ready within three days so that his armies might set forth against Wu under
the color of mourning. Two minor commanders Fan Jiang and Zhang Da
entered his tent and said, "The allotted period will have to be extended if we
are to arrange for white banners and white armors." Zhang Fei went into a
rage. He shrieked an order for them to be bound to a tree and given 50 lashes
crying, "If you fail, I will make a public example of your heads!" Zhang Da
said to Fan Jiang, "Better kill him than be executed. If fate wills us to live, he
will fall asleep drunk." That night Zhang Fei ordered wine and drank with his
officers. Before long, Zhang Fei fell into a drunken stupor. At the first watch
Zhang Da and Fan Jiang slipped into Zhang Fei's tent and plunged their
daggers into his belly. Zhang Fei gave a single cry and died.

## 背母进山

《东周列国志》中的故事。晋国重耳公子流亡在外，介子推等众臣跟随左右。众人饥饿，采摘植物叶充食，重耳不能下咽。介子推端来一碗肉汤，重耳食之味美，原来是介子推的股肉。子推说："孝子杀身以事其亲，忠臣杀身以事其君。"子推随重耳一十九年。当重耳为晋文公时，论功行赏。有人居功，有人争功。子推托病居家，甘受清贫，不求禄，无求于君。介子推老母说："你能为

## CARRYING HIS MOTHER TO THE MOUNTAIN

This is a story from the Records of the States of the Eastern Zhou Dynasty. In 770-476 BC, Prince Chong Er of the State of Jin lived in exile. Jie Zitui and other officials were constantly at his side. When they were hungry, they picked and ate leaves and fruit, but Chong Er could barely swallow them. Jie Zitui brought him a bowl of soup, which, upon tasting, Chong Er praised as delicious. It had actually been made from Jie Zitui's flesh. After being in exile for 19 years, Chong Er succeeded as Duke Wen of Jin, and he rewarded those who had helped him during those hard years. Some contended for merits and others asked for rewards. Jie Zitui excused himself, saying he was ill, and stayed at home, preferring to

廉士，我岂不能为廉士之母。"子推背老母进锦山，结庐于深谷之中。晋文公得知，率群臣进锦山寻访数日。晋文公认为子推是孝子，只要放火烧山，子推必背母出山。大火三日，发现子推母子死于枯柳之下。晋文公后悔不及，改锦山为介山，焚火之日定为"寒食节"。农历三月五日这一天，家家插柳于门，以招子推之魂。后来，成为清明节，各家祭祀祖先。

be poor rather than seek money or any reward. His mother said, "You are an honest and decent man of whom I am proud to be mother." Jie Zitui carried his mother on his back to the mountains, where they decided to live. When Duke Wen of Jin heard of this, he took his officials to Jin Mountain where they spent days looking for them. Duke Wen of Jin thought that as Jie Zitui was a filial son he would carry his mother away from the mountain if he set it on fire. Three days later they found Jie Zitui and his mother dead under a scorched willow tree. Duke Wen of Jin sorely regretted his actions, and changed the name of the mountain from Jin to Jie Mountain, and proclaimed the date on which the mountain was set alight as "Cold Food Festival". On the fifth day of the third month every household fixes a willow branch to their door to recall the spirit of Jie Zitui.

## 赵子龙单骑救主

在博望坡诸葛亮初用兵，以三千军马杀退曹兵十万。曹操亲统五十万大军奔新野、樊城而来。刘备知抵挡不住，领两县十数万宁死跟随的百姓退走。曹兵掩至，张飞保刘备且战且走。可怜十数万百姓，号哭之声震天动地。赵云保刘备二夫人，与敌厮杀至天

## ZHAO YUN SAVES THE YOUNG MASTER SINGLE-HANDEDLY

Zhuge Liang made his debut at Bowangpo and defeated 100,000 of Cao's troops with only 3,000 soldiers. Cao Cao led 500,000 troops to Xinye and Fancheng to seek revenge. Liu Bei knew that he could not stop the enemy's advance, and took over 100,000 people from the two counties along with his army on their retreat. As Cao's army approached, Zhang Fei escorted Liu Bei on his escape route. Zhao Yun was escorting two ladies of Liu Bei's court, and fought the enemy till the next morning. He

明，不见甘、糜二夫人。赵云杀进曹营，救出甘夫人，
复又冲进曹营寻糜夫人。寻至一井边，见糜夫人身受重
伤。糜夫人希望赵云能将刘备之子救出，见他父面，遂
投井而死。赵云将阿斗抱护在怀，绰枪上马，杀死曹营
名将五十余员，血染征袍，直透重围，救出幼主。这是
《三国演义》中第四十一回故事。

then discovered that the two ladies had disappeared, and went to
Cao's camp look for them. He first rescued Lady Gan, then found
Lady Mi at the side of a well, badly wounded. Lady Mi begged
Zhao Yun to save the life of Liu Bei's son and take him to his
father, and then jumped down the well to her death. Zhao Yun
placed A Dou, Liu Bei's son, inside his robes and mounted his
horse. He killed over 50 generals in Cao's camp, broke through a
tight encirclement, thus saving the young master. His clothes
were stained red with blood.

## 七星坛诸葛亮借东风

曹操率百万大军，连营三百余里，要过江攻打东吴。刘备派诸葛亮过江帮助东吴破曹。东吴都督周瑜想用火攻。一日，立于山顶，忽然望后而倒，口吐鲜血。原来农历十一月天气刮西北风，火攻破曹岂不烧了自己。诸葛亮知道其意，便写下十六个字："欲破

## ON THE SEVEN STAR ALTAR ZHUGE LIANG SUPPLICATES THE WIND

Cao Cao had led hundreds of thousands of troops pitching camps for a distance of over 150 kilometers, and was about to cross the Yangtze River to attack the Wu Kingdom. Liu Bei sent Zhuge Liang to the Wu to help them defeat Cao Cao. Zhou Yu, the chief commander of Wu, planned to use fire in his attack. One day, as Zhou Yu stood on the top of a hill, he suddenly fell over backward and spit blood. He was worried about attacking Cao Cao with fire, because in the eleventh month of the Chinese lunar calendar the northwest winds constantly blow, and he feared the fire

曹公，宜用火攻，万事俱备，只欠东风。"诸葛亮又说："在南山建一七星坛，我在坛上作法，可借三日三夜东风。"农历十一月二十日，东吴准备好火船，安排好兵马。是日近夜，微风不动。周瑜说："隆冬之时，怎得东风乎？"将近三更，风声响，东南风起。周瑜得东风火烧曹军。这是《三国演义》中第四十九回故事。

might blow back and consume Wu. Upon hearing this, Zhuge Liang wrote sixteen words, "To break Cao's back, with fire we attack. Everything is set, save the east wind we lack!" Zhuge Liang said, "By erecting a Seven Star Altar on the Southern Screen Hills, I will work certain charms to borrow three days and three nights of southeast wind." On the twentieth day of the eleventh month of the Chinese lunar calendar, the Wu Kingdom had already prepared fireboats and prepared its army for battle. Late that night there was no sign of a southwest wind to be seen. Zhou Yu said, "There can be no east wind in the dead of winter." At the third watch, a stiff gale blew up from the southeast. With the help of the southeast wind, Zhou Yu successfully used fire to defeat Cao's army.

## 滴翠亭宝钗戏彩蝶

《红楼梦》中第二十七回故事。农历四月二十六日是芒种节。按中国古代风俗，要设摆各色礼物，祭祀花神。大观园中女孩子们一早起来，用花瓣柳枝编成轿马等物系在每一棵树上或花上。众小姐和丫鬟们在园内玩耍，独不见林黛玉。宝钗便到潇湘馆来找。忽见前面一双玉色蝴蝶，大如团扇，一上一下迎风翩跹，十分有趣，遂向袖中取出扇子来，向草地下来扑，一直跟到池中滴翠亭上，香汗淋漓，娇喘细细。图中为宝钗扑蝶情景。

## BAOCHAI PLAYS WITH BUTTERFLIES AT THE DRIPPING EMERALD PAVILION

This is a story from Chapter Twenty-Seven of A Dream of Red Mansions. The twenty-sixth day of the fourth month of the Chinese lunar calendar is the Grain in Beard Festival. According to Chinese tradition, various gifts are laid on a table in worship of the god of money and flowers. The girls in the Grand View Garden got up early. They weaved petals and willow branches into sedan-chair horses and tied them to each tree or flower. All the young misses and their maids played in the garden except Lin Daiyu. Baochai went to her house to see her. Suddenly she saw a pair of jade colored butterflies as big as a palm fan flying up and down against the wind. Fascinated by their dancing, Baochai took out her fan and tried to waft them towards the meadow. She followed them to the pond under the Dripping Emerald Pavilion, by which time she was already out of breath and bathed in sweat. This painting shows Baochai wafting the butterflies.

## 祢衡裸衣骂曹

《三国演义》中第二十三回故事。曹操要派一人去招安荆州刘表，有人推荐祢衡。曹操招衡至。礼毕，操不命坐，祢衡出言讽刺曹操，曹操生气，命祢衡充当鼓吏。衡不推辞，应声而去。次日，曹操大宴宾客，衡穿破衣，击"渔阳三挝。"音节殊妙，坐客听之，莫不慷慨流涕。左右喝曰："何不更衣！"衡当众脱下破衣，

## MI HENG STRIPS DENOUNCING CAO CAO

This is a story from Chapter Twenty-Three of The Three Kingdoms. Cao Cao wanted to send someone to Jingzhou to persuade Liu Biao to join him. Mi Heng was recommended. Cao Cao summoned Mi Heng, and after greeting Cao Cao, he was not offered a seat, so he intimated his displeasure at this to Cao Cao, who was not happy to hear it. He ordered Mi Heng to be a drum master, which Mi Heng did not refuse and left as soon as Cao Cao had uttered this order. The next day, Cao Cao held a banquet for his guests. Mi Heng came, dressed in shabby clothes and performed the "Triple Tolling of Yuyang." The tone and rhythm were superb and all the guests were moved to tears. Cao's attendants shouted at him, "Why don't you change your clothes?" at which Mi Heng stripped

裸体而立。坐客皆掩面，操叱曰："庙堂之上，何太无礼！"衡曰："欺君罔上，乃谓无礼！吾露父母之形，以显清白之体耳！"操曰："汝为清白，谁为污浊？"衡曰："汝不识贤愚，是眼浊；不读诗书，是口浊；不纳忠言，是耳浊；不通古今，是身浊；不容诸侯，是腹浊；常怀篡逆，是心浊也！吾乃天下名士，用为鼓吏，如此轻人也？"

stark naked before the audience. The guests hastily shielded their eyes. "How dare you be so rude in the imperial court?" Cao cried. Mi Heng replied, "To abuse one's lord, or to deceive the sovereign, is what I call 'rudeness.' I have kept the body my parents gave me free of blemish." "If you are so pure," Cao Cao demanded, "who is corrupt?" Mi Heng responded, "Your inability to distinguish between the able and the incompetent shows that your eyes are corrupt. Your failure to read Confucian classics shows that your mouth is corrupt. Your rejection of loyal advice shows that your ears are corrupt. Your ignorance of past and present shows that your whole being is corrupt. Your conflicts with the lords of the realm show that your stomach is corrupt. Your dream of usurpation shows that your mind is corrupt. How can you hold a man like me, a renowned scholar, in such contempt, by making me serve as a drum master?"

## 颜超求寿

晋代《搜神记》中的故事。管辂(lù)平原人，善用《易经》占卜。一日，管辂回到家乡，见少年颜超有夭亡之相，告之。颜超的父亲求管辂延长儿子寿命。管辂对颜超说："你准备好酒一杯，鹿肉一斤，明早五点到燕麦地南大桑树下，有二人下围棋。你给他们斟酒送肉，斟完为止。你只管跪拜，不要说话。"颜超照管辂

## YAN CHAO BEGS FOR LONGEVITY

This tale comes from the Stories of Immortals. Guan Lu from Pingyuan was able at telling fortunes using the Book of Changes. One day, Guan Lu returned to his hometown and recognized in the young man Yan Chao the look of one who was to die young, and immediately told him so. Yan Chao's father pleaded with Guan Lu to extend his son's life. Guan Lu said to Yan Chao, "Please prepare a pot of good wine and half a kilo of venison, and bring them to the oats field at five tomorrow morning. Under a large mulberry tree south of the oats field there will be two men playing chess. You must pour them wine and offer them meat till all the wine is

的话做了。坐在北面的看见颜超叱道："你在这里干什么？"坐在南面的说："吃了他的酒肉难道无情？"坐在北面的说："文书写了。"坐在南面的从坐在北面的手里借过文书，见颜超寿命十九岁，将九字用笔钩到前面，对颜超说："救你活到九十岁。"回来后，管辂对颜超说："坐在北面的是北斗星君，坐在南面的是南斗星君。"

gone. You need only to kowtow and not say a single word." The next day Yan Chao followed Guan Lu's instructions. The one sitting to the north saw Yan Chao and shouted, "What are you doing?" The one sitting at the south said, "How can you be so rude after accepting his wine and meat?" The one sitting to the north said, "It's set out on the document." The one sitting to the south took the document from the one sitting at the north and saw that Yan Chao's life span was nineteen years. He moved the "nine" character to front of "ten" with his pen and said to Yan Chao, "You have been saved to live till ninety." After Yan Chao returned from the field, Guan Lu told Yan Chao, "The one sitting at the north was the King of the Big Dipper, while the one at the south was the King of the South Dipper."

## 娥皇和女英

尧将皇位传给舜,又把二个女儿娥皇和女英许配给舜。二姐妹像
父亲一样爱民,帮助舜为百姓做了许多好事。后来历朝历代的皇
帝都把自己比作尧舜。舜在暮年体衰时,还关心百姓疾苦,到处
体察民情,死在南方苍梧。娥皇和女英闻知舜死它乡,星夜赶奔
君山。在南方的路上,二姐妹常常扶竹痛哭,泪水滴滴流洒在竹
子上,留下斑斑泪痕,这就是"斑竹"。不幸,她们在奔丧南渡
湘水时,遇暴风,船翻身亡。百姓为纪念这二位皇妃,又称斑竹
为"湘妃竹"。

## EHUANG AND NUYING

Yao passed his throne over to Shun and married his two daughters Ehuang
and Nuying to Shun. The two sisters loved their people just as their father
did, and helped Shun do a great deal of good for the common people.
Later emperors of all dynasties liked to consider themselves as a Yao or a
Shun. In his old age Shun was deeply concerned about the weal and woe
of the people. He traveled to gain experience of their lives and died at
Cangwu in the south. Hearing Shun had died in another country, Ehuang
and Nuying rushed to Mount Jun that night. On their way south, the two
sisters frequently stopped to rest, and wept in bamboo groves, shedding
their tears on the bamboo, which were later named "tear-stained bamboo."
Unfortunately they were caught in a storm when crossing the Xiang River.
Their boat capsized and the two were drowned. People called the tear-
stained bamboo "Xiangfei bamboo" in memory of the two imperial ladies.

## 许仙借伞

《白蛇传》中的故事。中国清明节正是四月天气，变化无常。这一天，中国人扫墓、祭祖、踏青。少年许仙也来到杭州西湖烧香。一片乌云飘过，接着就是连绵细雨。许仙赶忙租一只小船，躲进船仓。小船刚刚划动，一个白衣女子喊着搭船。许仙见两个女子淋湿了衣服，连忙让他们上船。许仙见白衣女子美如天仙，白衣女子见许仙少年英俊，便攀谈起来，原来白衣女子叫白娘子。船到湖岸，许仙让二女子在仓内稍等。一会儿，他借一把伞回来给白娘子。后人称道说，百年修得同船渡，结成一对美姻缘。

## XU XIAN BORROWS AN UMBRELLA

This is a story from The Tale of the White Snake. In April, at the time of the Pure Brightness Festival, the weather is changeable. This is the time when Chinese go to pay their respect to the dead at their tombs, worship their ancestors, and go for a spring outing. The young scholar Xu Xian made a trip to the West Lake in Hangzhou at this time to burn incense. Dark clouds blackened the sky and it started to rain. Xu Xian hurriedly rented a boat and sheltered in a cabin and started out across the lake. No sooner had the boat left the bank than a girl in white and her maid shouted at the boatman to give her a lift. Seeing that the two girls were already soaked to the skin with rain, Xu Xian stopped the boat and let them aboard. Xu Xian thought that the girl in white was as beautiful as a fairy, while the girl in white saw that Xu Xian was young and handsome. The two started to talk. The girl in white was called Lady White. When the boat reached the bank of the lake, Xu Xian asked the two girls to wait in the cabin. After a while, he borrowed an umbrella and gave it to Lady White. Hundreds of years later, it is now believed that a couple crossing the river in the same boat will have a happy marriage.

## 唐僧历经八十一难

《西游记》中第九十九回故事。唐僧师徒四人去西天取经，路经
十万八千里，历过八十次灾愆患难，取回五千零四十八卷真经，
运往大唐，又回到八百里通天河边。那大白赖头鼋浮出水面叫道：
"唐圣僧，这里来！"悟空笑道："老鼋，向年累你，今岁又得相
逢。"师徒四人又登上鼋背。那老鼋蹭开四足，踏水面如行平地，
行经多半日，将近东岸，忽然回头问曰："老师父，我向年曾央
见我佛如来问问，我还有多少年寿？"唐僧忘记此事，无言可答。
老鼋即知不曾替问，他就将身一晃，沉下水去。他师徒四人，通
皆落水。

## THE TANG PRIEST'S EIGHTY-FIRST ORDEAL

This is a story from Journey to the West. The Tang Priest and his disciples went
to the West for Buddhist scriptures. They traveled 54,000 kilometers and
endured eighty ordeals on their journey. Eventually they obtained 5,048 rolls of
scriptures, which they packed and took on horseback to the capital of Tang.
They once again came to the banks of the River of Heaven. "This way, Tang
Priest, this way!" shouted a big, white, scabby-headed soft-shelled turtle,
raising its head from the river. Sun Wukong smiled and said, "We troubled you
in the past, old turtle, and this year we meet again." The Tang Priest and his
disciples stepped on to the back of the turtle. The turtle surged across the water
as if his four feet were walking on flat land, and carried them toward the
eastern bank for the best part of a day. Suddenly the turtle turned its head and
asked, "Venerable master, several years ago I begged you to ask Tathagata
Buddha how long I would live." The Tang Priest had forgotten about this, and
so said nothing. When the turtle realized that the Tang Priest had not asked this
question, it shook its body and submerged, casting them into the river.

## 占旺相四美钓游鱼

《红楼梦》中第八十一回故事。一日，宝玉睡了中觉起来，甚觉无聊，便来到藕香榭来，远远听见李绮、邢岫烟的声音。宝玉忍不住，拾起一块小砖头儿，往那水里一撂，咕咚一声，那边的人都吓了一跳，原来还有探春、李纹在一块钓鱼。宝玉道："咱们大家今儿钓鱼占占谁的运气好。"四位小姐都分头下钩钓上一个。这才把鱼杆递给宝玉。宝玉道："我是要做姜太公的。"便走下石矶，坐在池边钓起来。岂知那水里的鱼看见人影儿，都躲到别处去了。

## THE FOUR BEAUTIES FISH IN THE POND TO TRY THEIR LUCK

This is a story from Chapter Eighty-One of A Dream of Red Mansions. One day, Baoyu had nothing to do after a nap and strolled toward the Scented Lotus Pavilion. In the distance he could hear the voices of Li Wen and Xing Youyan. Baoyu could not help but pick up a pebble and throw it in the water. The splashing sound frightened the people there, who were fishing together with Tanchun and Li Wen. Baoyu said, "Let's see who is lucky today if we all go fishing here together." After each of the four all caught a fish, they handed the fishing rod to Baoyu. "I will be the Duke of Jiang," said Baoyu. He walked down stairs and sat at the pond fishing. He could not know that all the fish had fled at seeing the reflection of a person in the pond.

## 鹬蚌相争

见《战国策·燕策》。一天，一只河蚌张开两片贝壳，在河岸上晒太阳。一只喜欢吃贝肉的鹬鸟想在蚌壳中啄取肉吃。蚌迅速合上贝壳，紧紧地夹往鹬嘴不放。鹬鸟说："快张开贝壳，放了我；否则两天不下雨，你要干死的。"河蚌说："我一张贝，你就要啄我的肉吃；你的嘴两天拔不出，也要饿死的。"老渔翁和小孙子走过来，将鹬蚌一起捉住。"鹬蚌相争，渔人得利"的故事，寓意深远。

## A SNIPE AND A CLAM GRAPPLE

This story is from Strategies of the Warring States Period—State of Yan. One day, a clam was basking in the sun with its shell open. A snipe, having a particular liking for shellfish, tried to peck at the clam. The clam snapped its shell shut and held the snipe's beak. The snipe said: "Open your shell at once and let me go, otherwise you will die of thirst in two days if it doesn't rain." Answered the clam, "You will peck at me if I open the shell, and you will also die of hunger in two days if you cannot extricate your beak. " Later a fisherman and his grandson walked over and caught both the snipe and the clam together. The moral of this story of the deadlock between the snipe and the clam and the fisherman who benefited from it is that an uncompromising struggle between two parties which causes both to suffer allows a third party to gain.

## 问路陈仓

故事发生在公元前206年前，楚汉相争的时候。韩信离开项羽投奔汉中刘邦，途中向老樵夫打听道路，才知，项羽为了阻止刘邦出兵，早将通往汉中的惟一栈道烧毁。韩信求助老人寻求其它道路。好心的老樵夫想起去往陈仓的路，那是他三十年前走过的一次险路，多年来再也无人敢走了。韩信将方向、路线牢牢地记在心中，谢过老丈，取路陈仓。韩信受到刘邦重用，任大将军，用明修栈道麻痹项羽，兵马暗渡陈仓，为刘邦取得天下。

## ASKING A WAY TO CHENCANG

This story took place in 206 BC when the states of Chu and Han were contending for supremacy. Han Xin left Xiang Yu and went to join Liu Bang in Hanzhong. At the halfway point of his journey he asked an old woodcutter the way, and found out that Xiang Yu had already burned down the only plank road leading to Hanzhong in order to prevent Liu Bang dispatching his troops there. Han Xin begged the old man to help him find another way. The kind-hearted woodcutter suddenly remembered that there was a road to Chencang. It was a dangerous road that he had traveled thirty years previously, but no one had dared to go there for years. Han Xin took note of the direction and the route, thanked the old man, and took the path to Chencang. Later, Han Xin was promoted to the rank of general by Liu Bang. He openly rebuilt the bridge while secretly moving his troops to Chencang along another route. Eventually, he helped Liu Bang set up the Han Dynasty.

## 《客 至》

是唐代著名诗人杜甫(712～770年)诗。当代中国人都知道李白、杜甫的名字。他的这首《客至》写于成都草堂。一天，老友崔县令路过来访，使杜甫欢喜不尽，感慨之余，写下这首诗。今收入唐诗三百首里。这首诗也反映了杜甫隐居成都的生活情景。全诗如下：

"舍南舍外皆春水，但见群鸥日日来。
花径不曾缘客扫，蓬门今始为君开。
盘飧市远无兼味，樽酒家贫只旧醅。
肯与邻翁相对饮，隔篱呼取尽余杯。"

## TO A GUEST

This is a poem written by Du Fu (712-770), a famous poet of the Tang Dynasty. It was written in his cottage at Chengdu, Sichuan. One day, the county magistrate Cui, his old friend, unexpectedly called by, to Du Fu's great joy. He was so pleased to see him that he composed this poem to express his feelings. It also reflects his secluded life in Chengdu. It is now one of the three hundred poems of the Tang Dynasty.

"Spring water winds around my cottage at north and south;
I see flocks of gulls coming day after day.
The footpath covered with fallen flowers is not swept for guests;
My wicket door has opened today especially for you.
Far from the market, I can only offer plain fare,
Being poor, I have only a pot of home brewed wine,
I would like to drink together with my neighbor,
I will call to him over the fence to come finish it with me."

## 王华买老

民间传说。相传公元964年前，宋朝，有个叫王华的孤儿，靠打鱼为生，为人勤劳善良。一天，他卖鱼回来，见一群人围着一个衣衫褴褛的老人，他喊着让大家买爹。有人笑他，有人骂他，有人投石打他。王华见老人可怜，自己又没爹，就当众磕头认爹，背老人回家，让媳妇认公公，让孩子认爷爷。老人吃饭讲究，没有多久，王华就开始变卖家里东西，供老人用饭。最后，不得不将一双儿女卖掉。即使如此，王华夫妇也没有一点怨言和不满。老人认为王华是他从小走失的亲儿子。原来，老人是皇帝的亲弟弟，国内有名的八千岁，特为找儿子化妆出来。

## WANG HUA BUYS THE OLD

This is a Chinese folk tale. It is said that in 960, during the Song Dynasty, there was an orphan named Wang Hua. He was very kind and diligent and made a living by fishing. One day, on his way home after selling his fish, he saw a group of people crowded around an old man in shabby clothes, who was crying out for someone to buy him as their father. Some laughed at him, some swore at him, and others threw stones. Wang Hua felt sorry for the old man. As he had no father, he approached the old man, kowtowed in front of all the people, and then took him home. He asked his wife to accept the old man as her father-in-law and his children to call him grandfather. The old man was fastidious about his food, so before long Wang Hua had begun to sell all his property in order to afford the food the old man desired. Eventually, he had to sell his children for food, but Wang Hua and his wife uttered not a word of complaint. The old man, who was actually the emperor's younger brother, had disguised himself as a poor man and gone to look for his lost son, and thought that Wang Hua was his real son whom he had lost during his childhood.

## 苏武牧羊

汉武帝时，中郎将苏武奉旨出使匈奴。匈奴单于了解苏武的才能，许高官厚禄要苏武投降，苏武不为所动；单于杀副使以死相威胁，苏武宁死不屈；单于折磨他，将他发配西伯利亚贝加尔湖牧羊十九载，苏武手持汉朝符节，不忘汉朝使命。后来，苏武的朋友，汉朝大将军李陵与匈奴作战被俘投降，来此告诉苏武，他的父亲已死，兄弟被杀，夫人改嫁，武帝年迈，朝政混乱，不如投降的好。苏武表示宁愿为汉室社稷而死，决不背叛列祖列宗。李陵无言可对。后人把苏武牧羊的经历，填词谱曲，词曲催人泪下，一直演唱到今天。

## SU WU HERDS SHEEP

During the reign of Emperor Wu of the Han Dynasty (140-88BC), Su Wu was sent as an envoy to the Huns by order of the emperor. Chanyu, the Hun chieftain, had heard of Su Wu's talent and intended to persuade him to surrender by offering him a high position and a handsome salary, but Su Wu refused. Changyu killed the deputy envoy as a threat, but Su Wu said he would rather die than submit. Eventually, Changyu tortured Su Wu and sent him to herd sheep in Lake Baikal, Siberia for nineteen years. Su Wu kept the Han court tally and never forgot his mission. Later, Su Wu's friend Li Ling, a grand general of the Han Dynasty, fought a battle against the Huns, who captured him. He went to Siberia and told Su Wu that his father had died, that his brother had been killed, and that his wife had remarried. He also told Su Wu that the emperor was getting old and the court was in chaos, and it would be better for him to surrender. Su Wu answered that he was willing to die for the Han court, and would never betray his native country and ancestors. Li Ling thereupon had nothing further to say. Hence, a poignant song about Su Wu's experience of herding sheep was written, which people still sing today.

## 贵妃出浴华清池

唐玄宗（712～742年）得贵妃杨玉环后，"后宫佳丽三千人，三千宠爱在一身"。与她日宴夜欢，也不理朝政了。玄宗常陪杨贵妃游玩骊山宫。每次来骊山，贵妃都要在华清池中沐浴，正是：

　　　　"春寒赐浴华清池，温泉水滑洗凝脂；
　　　　侍儿扶起娇无力，如是新承恩泽时。"

这幅画就是取意于杨贵妃沐浴的情景。

## LADY YANG COMES OUT OF A BATH AT HUAQING POOL

After Emperor Xuan Zong of the Tang Dynasty had taken Yang Yuhuan as his concubine, his love for the remaining three thousand beauties housed in the rear palaces seemed to center on one. He idled his time away with her at feasts and leisure pursuits, and totally neglected government affairs. Emperor Xuan Zong often accompanied Lady Yang on visits to Lishan Palace, where each time Lady Yang would ask to bathe at the Huaqing Pool there.

Taking a bath at Huaqing Pool by orders of the emperor in the early spring,
To wash away blemishes with the smooth hot spring water,
When I hold my tired beauty up,
It is the time to receive bounties and win favors.

This painting depicts Lady Yang bathing.

## 阿 英

《聊斋志异》中的故事。甘珏，庐陵人，父母早丧，靠兄抚养成人。一日，甘珏到郊野游玩，遇一十六七岁少女。少女向甘珏微笑说："你是甘家二郎吗！令尊曾为你我订婚，三日之间，当候佳音。"甘珏回家向兄嫂提及此事。其兄说："此言荒谬！父死时我已二十岁，父不曾说过。"三日后，其兄外出回家途中，见一

## AYING

This is a story from Strange Tales of the Make-Do Studio. Gan Jue from Luling was brought up by her brother after his parents died. One day, as Gan Jue strolled about in a suburb he ran into a girl aged sixteen or seventeen. "Are you the second son of the Gan family?" the girl asked Gan Jue, continuing, "Your father once arranged our marriage. I'll wait three days for your answer." Gan Jue returned home and mentioned this to his brother and sister-in-law. His brother said, "Nonsense! I was twenty when father died, but he never mentioned this." Three days later, as Gan Jue's elder brother was on his way home from an outing, he saw a girl

女子哭啼行走，其貌绝美，人世罕见。问她为何啼哭，她说："我叫阿英，曾许配甘家二郎。因家穷远迁。近日回来才知甘家言而无信，背弃前盟。"甘珏兄长见此女与弟弟真乃天生一对，就请阿英回家。原来阿英是甘珏父亲养的仙鹦鹉。甘珏四岁时，其父开玩笑地说："快去喂它，长大了给你做媳妇。"鹦鹉后来飞走，多年后回来了却这段姻缘。

weeping as she walked, and saw that she had a rare beauty. He went up to her and asked why she was crying. "My name is Aying," said the girl, "I was betrothed to the second Gan son. As my family is poor and had to move to a place far away from here, I could not return. Recently I came back and learned that the Gan's have broken their word." Gan Jue's elder brother saw that the girl and his brother were a born match, and invited Aying to his home. Aying was actually a parrot spirit raised by Gan Jue's father. When Gan Jue was four, his father had jokingly said to him, "Go and feed the parrot at once so that it can be your wife when you grow up." Later the parrot flew away. Several years went by, until she returned in human form to settle this marriage.

## 屯土山关云长约三事

关云长兵败，引兵屯于土山，曹兵团团将土山围住。曹操素爱云长武艺人材，欲得之以为己用，便派大将张辽前去说降。张辽劝云长留有用之身，以便保刘备二夫人，待得知刘备音信，即往投之不晚。关云长说："吾有三约，若丞相能从，我即去投降：一者，共扶汉室，不降曹操；二者，二嫂处请给养赡，一应上下人等，皆不许到门；三者，但知刘备去向，不管千里万里，便当辞去。"曹操答应了云长要求。后来关云长悬印、封金、过五关斩六将，投奔刘备。这是《三国演义》中第二十五回故事。

## GUAN YUNCHANG SETS THREE CONDITIONS AT TU HILL

This is a story from Chapter Twenty-Five of The Three Kingdoms. Guan Yunchang had been defeated and led his men to Tu Hill, which was surrounded by Cao's troops. Cao Cao had long admired Guan Yunchang's skill at martial arts and wanted him work for him, so he sent his general Zhang Liao to win him over. Zhang Liao urged Guan Yunchang to save his life in order to ensure the safety of the two ladies of Liu Bei's court. Guan Yunchang said, "I have three conditions, and if your prime minister agrees to them, I will submit. First, I have sworn to uphold the house of Han. I shall submit to the Emperor, not to Cao Cao. Second, the two ladies should be well treated. No one should be allowed to approach their door. Third, as soon as I learn of Liu Bei's whereabouts, I will leave for him no matter how far away it is." Cao Cao accepted Guan Yunchang's conditions. Later, Guan Yunchang hung his seal in the main hall, locked away all the gold and valuables, and left for Liu Bei after slaying six generals and breaching five passes.

## 尤三姐耻情归地府

宁国府亲戚尤三姐，古今绝色，看上了贾宝玉的朋友柳湘莲，声称非他不嫁。一日，贾琏在路上相遇湘莲提亲，湘莲将鸳鸯剑取出为信物。贾琏回京将宝剑交给三姐，三姐喜出望外，她已等他五年了。柳湘莲来京后，左思右想，后悔不该答应这门婚事。他认为贾府里除了两石头狮子干净，连猫儿狗儿都不干净。便找贾琏取祖上传下来的宝剑。三姐出屋，泪如雨下，左手将剑并鞘送与湘莲，右手回肘只往项上一横，自刎身亡。湘莲扶尸大哭，走出贾府，自己也一剑，将头发一挥而尽，跟一道士出家去了。这是《红楼梦》中第六十六回故事。

## THE THIRD SISTER YOU COMMITS SUICIDE

This is a story from Chapter Sixty-Six of A Dream of Red Mansions. The Third Sister You, a relative from Ning Mansion, was extremely pretty. She fell in love with Jia Baoyu's friend Liu Xianglian and claimed that she would not marry anyone but him. One day Jia Lian ran into Liu Xianglian and proposed the Third Sister You as a marriage partner for Xianglian. Xianglian took out his mandarin duck sword and asked Jia Lian to give it to the Third Sister You as a token. On returning home, Jia Lian gave the sword to the Third Sister You, who was overjoyed, as she had waited for Liu Xianglian for five years. Later Liu Xianglian went back to the capital city. He thought about this marriage to which he had committed himself, and started to have regrets. He thought that no one, even the cats and dogs in the Jia Mansion, was clean, apart from two stone lions. He went to see Jia Lian and asked him for the return of his ancestor's sword. The Third Sister You stepped out of her room weeping, her heart broken. She handed the scabbard to Liu with her left hand while drawing out the sword with her right, lifting her elbow to cut her own throat. Xianglian cried bitterly over her body. He left the Jia Mansion, cut off all his hair, and left with a Taoist. From that time on, he lived as a priest.

## 《牡丹亭》艳曲警芳心

贾元春省亲后，想起大观园必定敬谨封锁，岂不寥落。遂下一道谕，命妹妹们去居住，命宝玉随进去读书。三月中旬一天，宝玉携一套《西厢记》在桃花树下阅读。正看到"落花成阵"时，黛玉来到。她接过书，从头看去越看越爱，自觉词藻警人，余香满口。宝玉有事回房。黛玉一人走到梨香院墙外，忽听墙内笛韵悠扬，歌声婉转，戏班子正在排《牡丹亭》。且听唱道："良辰美景奈何天，赏心乐事谁家院。"不觉点头自叹。又听唱道："则为你如花美眷，似水流年……"不觉心动神摇，如醉如痴。这是《红楼梦》中第二十三回故事。

# A SONG FROM PEONY PAVILION DISTRESSES A TENDER HEART

This is a story from Chapter Twenty-Three of A Dream of Red Mansions. After Jia Yuanchun, an imperial concubine, had been home for a visit, she thought that keeping the Grand View Garden locked and allowing no one to enter was a waste, so she issued an order whereby her sisters might live there and Baoyu could also study there. One day in mid March, Baoyu took a copy of The Western Chamber to the garden and was reading it under a peach tree. As he reached the line "Red petals fall in drifts", Lin Daiyu came. Baoyu had something to do and went back to his room. She took the book from him and read it. The more she read the more enthralled she became. She felt as if the sheer beauty of the language had left a sweet taste in her mouth. As Daiyu strolled towards Pear Fragrance Court, she heard the sweet sounds of a flute and singing over the wall. A theatrical troupe was rehearsing the drama "the Peony Pavilion". Hearing the lines "what an enchanting sight on this fine morning, but who is there that takes delight in the spring?" she nodded and sighed. As she listened to the lines "for you are as fair as a flower, and youth is slipping away like flowing water..."she could not help but let her heart be carried away by them.

## 老子出关

老子姓李名聃，是中国道教创始人，哲学奠基人，政治家，理论家。春秋时的孔子也经常向老子请教。晚年，老子骑着一头青牛西行，来到函谷关。守关的将领尹喜请老子为文武官员讲道。老子的道太过深奥，就是孔子51岁时请教老子，都不懂"道"的真正含义，又何况这些官员，便请他留下文字。老子写下五千余字的《道德经》出关练道养命去了，活了二百余岁。西汉年间朝野上下背诵《道德经》。即成道教，以《道德经》为教的宗旨。图为老子出关情景。

## LAOZI EXITS THE HANGU PASS

Laozi's real name was Li Dan, and he was the founder of Chinese Taoism and philosophy. He was a great thinker, politician and theorist during the Spring and Autumn Period (770-476 BC), at which time Confucius often consulted him. In his later years, Laozi rode his black ox to the west and arrived at the Hangu Pass. The commanding general, Yin Xi, invited him to lecture the officers and generals. Laozi's Taoism was so profound that even Confucius had, at the age of 51, once asked him about the real meaning of Tao. The officers at the Hangu Pass asked Laozi to write the meaning of Tao. Laozi wrote his spiritual classic, The Scripture of Ethics, in over 5,000 characters and went on through the pass. He practiced his doctrines and lived for over 200 years. In the Western Han Dynasty, all the people in the court and the locality recited The Scripture of Ethics. The Doctrine of Five Pecks of Rice is another term for Taoism whose principle is based on The Scripture of Ethics. This painting shows Laozi exiting the pass.

## 《月下独酌》

李白（701～762年），唐代伟大诗人。这首《月下独酌》几乎人人会吟。古今一些文人，有的借诗抒情，有的借诗伤感，有的赏玩词句。图为李白举杯邀明月的情景。诗的全文如下：

"花间一壶酒，独酌无相亲。
举杯邀明月，对影成三人。
月既不解饮，影徒随我身。
暂伴月将影，行乐须及春。
我歌月徘徊，我舞影零乱。
醒时同交欢，醉后各分散。
永结无情游，相期邈云汉。

## DRINKING ALONE UNDER THE MOON

Li Bai (701-762) was a great poet of the Tang Dynasty. The following poem is very popular and most Chinese people can recite it. Literary men today and in the past like to express their emotions, and to savor the verses they have written by chanting their poetry. This painting depicts Li Bai toasting the moon. The whole poem reads:

"A pot of wine among the flowers from which I drink alone.
I raise my cup to toast the bright moon,
Who makes it, me ,and my shadow into three persons,
The moon does not know how to drink her share,
In vain my shadow follows me here and there.
With them for the time being,
I spend a merry life before spring goes by.
The moon lingers as I sing,
And my shadow disperses at my dancing steps.
We remain cheerful and happy while awake,
We part and go each our own ways when drunk.
Our friendship will last forever,
Next time we will meet beyond the stars above.

**153**

## 嫘祖养蚕

中国远古时代，大约在公元前26世纪，黄帝娶西陵氏之女为妻，名叫嫘(lei)祖。嫘祖好游，因此见多识广。她在家操劳家务，出外帮助黄帝处理政务。还学会了养蚕，用蚕丝织绢。图为嫘祖教百姓采桑养蚕的情景。嫘祖死在出外的路途中，被天帝封为行神。

## LEIZU ENGAGES IN SERICULTURE

In about 26th century BC in ancient China, the Yellow Emperor married the daughter of Lady Xiling who was named Leizu. Leizu was fond of traveling, and so was rich in knowledge and experience. She managed household affairs, helped the Yellow Emperor handle government affairs, and learned sericulture and how to weave silk. This painting shows Leizu teaching sericulture. She died on one of her journeys, and was conferred the title God of Travel by the Emperor of Heaven.

## 祝鸡公

在晋朝（265～420年），河南洛阳有个很有学识的祝公，终生养鸡，在尸乡北山脚下，数十年以鸡为伴。他养的千余只鸡都有一个漂亮的名字，只要祝公高呼鸡名，那只鸡便像他的孩子一样，从远处应声而至。他养鸡闻名，大家习惯称他为祝鸡公。几百里外的人都来向他求教养鸡方法，祝鸡公总是热心传授。祝鸡公死后，人们为了纪念他，就以他的姓氏"祝"呼唤鸡。每逢喂鸡的时候，人们便喊"祝、祝、祝、祝"，鸡群就会闻"祝"而至。

## ZHU JIGONG (COCK ZHU GONG)

In the Jin Dynasty (265-420) lived a learned man named Zhu Gong in Luoyang, Henan. He had raised chickens all his life and lived at the northern foot of Shixiang Mountain for several decades. He had over one thousand chickens and each had a beautiful name. Whenever Zhu Gong called a cock's name, it would answer him in the distance and run to him like his own child. He was so well known for his chicken raising that people called him Zhu Jigong (Cock Zhu Gong). People from several hundred kilometers away often came to consult him on methods of raising chickens, and Zhu Jigong was always willing to teach them. After he died, people used his surname Zhu to call their chickens in his memory. At feeding time, people call "Zhu, zhu, zhu zhu", and all the chickens come as if summoned.

## 憨湘云醉卧芍药裀

贾宝玉生日，姊妹和丫鬟们前来祝寿，祝出四个寿星，还有薛宝琴、邢岫烟和平儿。于是宝玉就同众姊妹连同各人身边的丫鬟，摆出四桌酒席，热闹起来。雅坐无趣，众人行起酒令，史湘云乱了酒令，被罚一杯，犯令规，被罚一杯。在吃鸭头的时候又说："这鸭头，不是那丫头，头上那讨桂花油。"众人发笑，丫头们不饶她，又罚一杯。这里没人管束，任意取乐，十分热闹，倏然不见了湘云。原来湘云吃醉了酒，躺在山后一块青板石凳上，业已香梦沉酣，四周芍药花飞了一身，口内犹作睡语说着酒令。

## XIANGYUN SLEEPS TIPSILY AMONG PEONIES

This is a story from Chapter Sixty-Two of A Dream of Red Mansions. On Baoyu's birthday, all his sisters and their maids came to congratulate him. They then found out that it was also the birthday of Xue Baoqin, Xing Xiuyan and Ping'er, so Baoyu decided to have a feast on four tables and celebrate with his sisters and their maids. They thought just feasting quietly was dull, so they started to play drinking games. Shi Xiangyun broke the rules and was fined by being made to drain a cup. She then made another mistake, and was forced to drink another cup. As they were eating a duck's head, Xiangyun said, "This duck's head is not that of a serving-maid. How can its head be smeared with oil of osmanthus?" Everyone laughed, and the maids forced her to drink another cup. As there was nobody to control them, they enjoyed themselves just as they pleased. Suddenly they found Xiangyun was missing. She was drunk and had gone to lay on a stone behind an artificial mountain. She was sound asleep and covered with peony petals that had fallen over her body. She was still murmuring lines for forfeits in her sleep.

## 《登鹳鹊楼》

王之涣（688～742年）是武则天和唐玄宗时代的诗人。鹳鹊楼，顾名思义，是鹳鹊栖落的地方，建于黄河之滨，楼高三层，为唐代风景胜地。当时，许多文人墨客留字于此。200年后，河床积淤，河水改道，淹没了唐代名楼，只留下了不朽的诗篇。王之涣这首二十字诗，语言简朴。前十个字把落日、大山、大河、大海一笔写出，气象万千，风景壮丽；后十个字寓意深远，丰有哲理，使人联想翩翩，称得起千古绝句。全诗如下：

"白日依山尽，黄河入海流。
欲穷千里目，更上一层楼。"

## ON GUANQUE TOWER

Wang Zhihuan (688-742) was a poet at the time of the reigns of Empress Wu Zetian and Emperor Xuan Zong of the Tang Dynasty. Guanque Tower was a place for storks and magpies to perch. It was built on the banks of the Yellow River in three stories and was one of the scenic spots of the Tang Dynasty. At that time many literary men came and left their poems here. Two hundred years later the river bed silted up, forcing the river to change its course. It flooded and submerged this famous tower of the Tang Dynasty, but poems written about it passed down from generation to generation. This poem, written by Wang Zhihuan and having only twenty characters, is simple and succinct. The first ten characters describe the magnificent sunset views, high mountains, large rivers and vast seas, while the last ten characters have philosophical profundity. They stimulate the imagination and are considered some of the best lines ever written. The poem reads:

"The sun beyond the mountains glows;
The Yellow River seawards flows.
You can enjoy a grander sight
By climbing to a greater height."

## 衾枕昧节候，褰开暂窥临

二句出自谢灵运的《登池上楼》。谢灵运为南北朝时著名诗人，曾赴任永嘉为太守。在任上重病卧床，大病初愈，使女搀扶上楼，命挂起帷帐，推开南窗，原来季节已变了。他倾耳聆听波澜之声，举目远眺青山，春风已吹走了寒冷，池塘绿草如茵，园柳枝头的鸟儿也变声歌唱了。全诗描写细腻：

"徇禄反穷海，卧疴对空林。
衾枕昧节候，褰开暂窥临。
倾耳聆波澜，举目眺岖嵚。
初景革绪风，新阳改故阴。
池塘生春草，园柳变鸣禽。"

This painting illustrates the scene described in the poem Climbing the Tower on a Pond written by Xie Lingyun, a famous poet of the Southern and Northern Dynasties. He was originally governor of Yongjia, but fell seriously ill during his term of office and stayed in bed for an extended period. Upon his recovery, he climbed the tower with the help of his home maid. He asked the maid to lift the curtains and open the southern window, and then realized that the seasons had already changed. He listened to the sound of waves and looked at the green hills in the distance. The spring breeze had blown away the cold and turned the grass around the pond green, and birds sang on the branches of the willow in the garden.

## 东郭先生

中国古代寓言故事。晋国有个东郭先生，为人好善。有一天，他骑头毛驴，驮着一些书去讲学。正走着，一头狼奔到驴前，急喘着说："先生，我是不吃人的狼，救救我吧！"东郭先生把口袋里的书倒进草丛，把狼装进口袋，骗过了追杀狼的猎人，又放出了狼。狼说："刚才差点把我闷死。"说着，张开大嘴，要吃东郭先生。东郭大喊救命，走来一个扛锄老汉。东郭先生和狼对老汉各说各理，老汉说不相信狼能钻进这么小的口袋里。狼就再次钻进去给老汉看。老汉立刻把口袋系上，抡起锄头把狼打死。老汉对东郭先生说："人对狼行善，狼是要吃掉人的！"

## MASTER DONGGUO

This is an ancient Chinese fable. In 475-221 BC in the State of Jin lived a soft-hearted person named Dongguo. One day, he was riding his donkey carrying some of his teaching books. A wolf suddenly ran in front of the donkey, gasping for breath, saying: "Master, I am not the kind of wolf that eats people. Please save me!" Master Dongguo emptied his books into a bush and let the wolf get into the sack. He sent the hunter away and set the wolf free. The wolf said: "I came close to being choked to death," upon which it opened its mouth with the intent of eating Master Dongguo. "Help, help!" shouted Dongguo. An old farmer with a hoe over his shoulder came along. Dongguo and the wolf explained each of their stories to him. The old man said he did not believe that the sack was big enough for the wolf. The wolf proved it to the man by getting into the sack again. The old man quickly tied up the sack, swung his hoe and beat the wolf to death. Then he told Dongguo: "People who are soft-hearted to a wolf will be eaten by it."

## 乱蟠桃大圣偷丹

一朝，王母娘娘在瑶池中做蟠桃盛会，要宴请西天佛老、菩萨、圣僧、罗汉及众神仙。大圣听说没有请他，便来到瑶池。他闻到一阵酒香，止不住口角流涎，忙拔下毫毛，变成众多瞌睡虫，投向瑶池内外一千人众。众仙丢了执事，都去瞌睡。大圣拿了些百味八珍，佳肴异品，就着缸，挨着瓮，放开量，痛饮一番。他吃醉了酒，竟奔兜率宫而来。见丹房无人，炉左右安放着五个葫芦，里面都是炼就的金丹，就吃几丸尝新。他觉得好吃，索性把那葫芦都倾出来，如吃炒豆相似，把丹都吃了。这是《西游记》中第五回故事。

## THE GREAT SAGE STEALS THE PILLS OF IMMORTALITY AFTER DISTURBING THE PEACH BANQUET

This is a story from Chapter Five of Journey to the West. One day the Queen Mother arranged a peach banquet by the Jade Pool and invited the Buddha of the Western Heaven, Bodhisattvas, holy monks, arhats, and the venerable immortals to a feast of peaches. Learning that he was not invited, the Great Sage came straight to the Jade Pool himself. As soon as he smelt the fragrant fermentation of the lees, the Great Sage could not stop himself from drooling. He quickly pulled several hairs from his body, and made them change into sleep-inducing insects that he threw at all the immortals in and around the Jade Pool. The immortals soon dropped their symbols of office and fell asleep. The Great Sage grabbed the rare delicacies and exotic foods, and went under the portico to drink from all the vats and pots until he was drunk. He then made his way to the Doshuai Palace. Seeing that there was no one there but that there were five gourds full of golden pills of refined elixir on either side of the stove, the Great Sage tasted some. When he found they were delicious, he emptied all the gourds and ate them up as if he were eating fried beans.

## 景阳冈武松打虎

前面讲过三碗不过冈。武松绰起哨棒，过景阳冈。他正走着，酒力发作，见一块大青石，却待要睡，只听树后扑地一声响，跳出一只吊睛白额大虫来。那大虫一扑，一掀，一剪，三般捉不着武松，再吼一声扑来。武松一棒打急了，打在枯树上，棒折两截。那大虫性起，扑将过来。武松只一跳，退了十步远，那大虫两只前爪搭在武松面前。武松两手揪住大虫，两只脚望大虫面门、眼睛只顾乱踢。他又抽出右手，尽平生之力，只顾打。打到五六十拳，那大虫眼里、口里、鼻子里、耳朵里迸出鲜血，气已没了。这是《水浒传》中第二十三回故事。

## WU SONG KILLS A TIGER ON MOUNT JINGYANG

This is the continuation of the story from Chapter Twenty-Three of Outlaws of the Marsh from page 44. Wu Song picked up his cudgel and strode off towards Mount Jingyang. As he walked, the wine began to burn inside his body. He saw a large rock and was about to sleep on it. There was suddenly a roar from behind a tree and a huge tiger with a white forehead and bulging eyes jumped out. When its three methods of spring, swipe and slash all failed to kill its victim, the tiger became furious. It roared again and whirled around. Wu Song swung his cudgel at the tiger, but in his haste he struck an old tree and it broke in two. The tiger was still more enraged, and it charged Wu Song, who leapt back ten paces, so that the tiger landed with its front paws in front of him. Wu Song grasped the tiger's ruff and kicked its forehead and eyes again and again. He then freed his right hand and pounded the tiger with all his strength. After fifty or sixty blows the tiger was bleeding from its eyes, mouth, and nose and soon died.

## 苦肉计黄盖受刑

黄盖乃东吴三朝老臣，愿前去曹营诈降。周瑜说："不受些苦，曹操如何肯信？"黄盖说："我受孙氏厚恩，虽肝脑涂地，亦无怨悔。"次日，周瑜鸣鼓大会诸将于帐下。周瑜说："操引百万之众，非一日可破。诸将各领三个月粮草，准备御敌。"黄盖说："若是这个月破了，便破，若是破不了，只可北面而降。"周瑜大怒，喝令速斩黄盖。众官苦苦求求。周瑜看在众官面皮，打黄盖一百脊杖。只打得黄盖鲜血迸流，昏死过去。黄盖伤中写信降曹，后来才趁曹操不备，火烧曹营。

## HUANG GAI IS FLOGGED FOLLOWING A TRICK

Huang Gai was a Wu official in the Three Kingdoms. One day, Huang Gai said to Zhou Yu: "I'm willing to pretend to surrender to Cao's camp." Zhou Yu asked: "What credibility will you have if you bear no wounds?" Huang Gai replied: "I would freely and willing strew my innards on the ground if necessary." The next day Zhou Yu sounded the drums, convening a general assembly of his commanders outside his tent. Zhou Yu said: "Cao Cao's millions of troops will not be defeated in one day. All of you take three months' rations and prepare to defend our territory." Huang Gai came forward and said: "If we can defeat them this month, then let's do it. If not, let's bow to the north and surrender." Zhou Yu exploded in fury and ordered to have Huang Gai executed. All commanders begged Zhou Yu to be lenient. In the face of the strenuous protests of his commanders, Zhou Yu instead ordered that Huang Gai be flogged one hundred strokes across the back. Poor Huang Gai was whipped severely and fainted. Huang Gai then wrote Cao Cao a letter of surrender, which enabled the later plan to burn down Cao's camp to be expedited, through his secretly communicated information.

## 穆桂英挂帅

《杨家将》中的故事。杨家一门忠心报国。杨令公、杨家八郎、杨宗保等三代人都为国捐躯。杨门只剩一群寡妇和幼童，解甲归田。一日，穆桂英一双儿女杨文广和杨金花进京游玩，见校场正在比武。原来，辽兵进犯中原，连破宋国重镇。宋王朝无一人敢领兵抗敌。皇帝只好贴出招贤的告示。奸臣王强命儿子王伦下校场，夺得帅印，以便通辽叛国。文广、金花少年气盛，下校场比武，金花箭射金钱眼，文广与王伦比试，杀了王伦，捧回帅印。此时，穆桂英已年过半百，见帅印热泪盈眶，痛责文广、金花无知，但还是以国家为重，挂帅出征破辽。

## MU GUIYING ASSUMES COMMAND

This is a story from Generals of the Yang Family. The Yang family members were all patriots. Three generations of the Yang family—the father, eight sons and the grandson Yang Zongbao all gave their lives for their country, leaving only young women, widows and children family members. One day, Mu Guiying went to the capital city to visit her son Yang Wenguang and daughter Yang Jinhua. She saw what appeared to be a martial arts competition being held on the drill ground. Liao troops had invaded the Central Plains once more and captured several major Song cities, but no one in the Song court dared to command its army to resist them, so the emperor posted a notice asking for one willing to do so. The treacherous court official Wang Qiang asked his son Wang Lun to participate in the competition and seize the commander's seal in order to betray the country to the State of Liao. Yang Wenguang and Yang Jinhua were young and aggressive. They went to the drill ground to join in the competition. Yang Jinhua hit the golden thread eye target with her bow and arrow and Yang Wenguang competed in martial skills with Wang Lun. He succeeded in killing him and winning the commander's seal. At this time, Mu Guiying was over fifty years old. Seeing the seal she could not stop tears from filling her eyes, and severely rebuked her two children for their ignorance. However for the sake of the country, she assumed command and went out to defeat the Liao army.

## 典韦救曹身亡

西凉将张绣每天设宴请操。一日操醉，要寻妓女。曹操侄子便把城内张济之妻，张绣婶娘接来。张绣得知，深恨曹操辱他太甚。请曹操随身护卫大将典韦到寨，殷勤待酒，使尽醉而归，暗中偷走典韦八十斤铁戟。四更火起，张绣兵到，曹操忙唤典韦。典韦正在醉卧，听喊声跳起来掣步兵卒腰刀，身无片甲，砍死二十余人，逼张绣军马方退，步兵又到，典韦双手提着两个军士迎敌，又击死八九人。典韦身受数中枪，背上中枪而死。曹操才能逃走。这是《三国演义》中第十六回故事。

THE STORIES BEHIND THE LONG CORRIDOR PAINTINGS AT THE SUMMER PALACE

## DIAN WEI DIES RESCUING CAO CAO

This is a story from Chapter Sixteen of The Three Kingdoms. Zhang Xiu, a Xiliang general gave a feast for Cao Cao every day. One day, Cao Cao was drunk and asked that courtesans from the city be brought to him. Cao Cao's nephew brought Zhang Ji's wife and Zhang Xiu's aunt to him from the city. When Zhang Xiu heard of this, he hated Cao Cao for humiliating him. He invited Dian Wei, Cao's personal guard, to dine, entertained him lavishly, and sent him home late and drunk. In the meantime he ordered his man to steal the forty kilo iron halberd. At the fourth watch, fire broke out and Zhang Xiu's army arrived. Cao Cao called for Dian Wei. Dian Wei was sleeping when he heard the call. He leaped to his feet, grabbed a sword from a foot soldier and went out to fight without armor. He cut down over twenty enemies and forced Zhang Xiu's horsemen to withdraw. At this moment, Zhang Xiu's foot soldiers came. Dian Wei picked up two enemy corpses and wielded them as weapons, felling eight or nine more enemies. Dian Wei was shot with several spears and died after being attacked from behind. Dian Wei's valiant defense enabled Cao Cao to escape.

## 秉烛夜游

唐代诗人李白，不仅写了很多传世的好诗，而且还写了不少抒情散文；《春夜宴诸从弟桃花园序》就是其中一篇。其文大概的意思是：天地是万物赖以投宿的旅店，光阴从百代人身边匆匆而过，飘浮的人生如梦，欢乐又能有几何？所以古人秉灯夜游寻乐，是多么有道理啊！李白的原文是：

"夫天地者，万物之逆旅也；光阴者，百代之过客也。
而浮生若梦，为欢几何？古人秉烛夜游，良有以也！"

## A NIGHT TOUR WITH A CANDLE

The Tang poet Li Bai not only wrote popular poetry but also lyric prose, among which was "Preface to a Spring Night Feast for Brothers at the Peach Flower Garden." The general idea expressed is that heaven and earth are an inn for the ten thousand creatures; time passes by swiftly throughout hundreds of generations; human life is like a dream and how many happy times come along? Therefore, how reasonable it was for ancients to take a night tour with a candle!

## 江东二乔

诸葛亮为激周瑜抗曹，对周瑜说："操本好色之徒，久闻江东乔公有二女，大乔二乔，曹发誓愿得江东二乔，置之铜雀台，以乐晚年，虽死无恨矣。何不以千金买此二女，差人送与曹操？操得二女，必班师矣。"周瑜问诸葛亮有何证验，操欲得二乔？诸葛亮就把曹操新造铜雀台赋背诵了一遍。周瑜大怒，离座指北骂曰："老贼欺吾太甚，吾与老贼誓不两立！"原来大乔是孙权哥哥孙策之妻，二乔是周瑜之妻。这是《三国演义》中第四十四回故事。

## THE TWO QIAO DAUGHTERS IN THE SOUTHLAND

This is a story from Chapter Forty-Four of the Three Kingdoms. In order to arouse Zhou Yu's indignation and resist Cao Cao, Zhuge Liang said to him, "Cao Cao is fond of beautiful women. He has known for a long time that the Southland patriarch Qiao has two daughters, elder Qiao and younger Qian. He has sworn to possess the Southland's two Qiao daughters and install them in the Bronze Bird Tower so that he may have pleasure in his later years and die without regret. Why not buy these two girls with a thousand pieces of gold and dispatch someone to deliver them to Cao? Once Cao has them, he will return to the capital." Zhou Yu asked Zhuge Liang to give him some evidence of Cao's desire to possess these two daughters. Zhuge Liang recited the "Bronze Bird Tower Rhapsody" for the new tower built by Cao Cao to Zhou Yu. Zhou Yu flew into a rage. He left his seat and pointed north cursing, "Old traitor! Rogue! You and I cannot share footing on this earth, this I swear." The elder Qiao was actually the wife of Sun Ce, Sun Quan's brother, and the younger Qiao was Zhou Yu's wife.

## 关云长义释曹操

农历十一月二十日夜，东吴火船乘东南风，四下里撞入曹军水寨。但见三江水面，火逐风飞，一派通红，漫天彻地，曹操叫苦连声。大将张辽保曹操离船，又遭东吴和刘备兵马接连劫杀伏击。来到华容道，曹百万兵马只剩三百余骑，人皆饥饿，马尽困乏，衣甲湿透，军旗不整。曹操正在大笑周瑜、诸葛亮不会用兵时，一声炮响，大将关云长率五百校刀手摆开。曹操只好求关云长念在往日情义上，能放过他。关云长见曹军惶惶皆欲垂泪，心中不忍，要放曹操走，可是想到军令，又大喝一声，曹军皆下马，哭拜于地。云长更不忍，长叹一声，皆放其生。

## GUAN YUNCHANG RELEASES CAO CAO

On the night of the twentieth day of the eleventh month of Chinese lunar calendar, fiery boats from the south rode with the wind and rammed into Cao's riverside camp. The water surface where the three rivers joined was red with the reflection of flames rising to the heavens from the earth. Cao Cao cried out in anguish. General Zhang Liao helped Cao Cao down from the ship, but soon they came under attack from Liu Bei's army. When they reached the Huarong Trail, only three hundred soldiers out of millions of troops were left. They were all starved and exhausted, their clothes were wet with sweat, and not one had clothing and armor intact. At the moment when Cao Cao had laughed at Zhou Yu and Zhuge Liang as incapable of using troops, a call to advance echoed and five hundred expert swordsmen led by General Gran Yunchang flanked the road. Cao Cao pleaded with Guan to let him go for the sake of favors and kindness in the past. At the sight of Cao's men distracted and Cao himself on the verge of tears, Guan Yunchang softened and swung his mount away to let Cao Cao pass, but then suddenly remembered his military orders and gave a powerful shout. Cao Cao and his soldiers all dismounted, prostrated themselves, and wept. Guan Yunchang could no longer stand it. He heaved a long sigh and let Cao Cao and his remaining troops escape.

## 灌水得球

北宋年间，山西介休文彦博，为官50余年，历经四朝，官至宰相，后封为潞国公。然而他经常和布衣朋友们聚会饮酒，如平民百姓一般，从不提半个官字。灌水得球就是文彦博小时候的故事。彦博小时候聪明伶俐。一天，他和小朋友们玩球，不小心将球踢进树洞里。有的小朋友用手掏，洞深，手够不着；有的有木棍夹，球圆，怎么也夹不住，夹住了又滚掉了。大家正在着急，彦博端来一盆水，倒进树洞，球浮出树洞口。小朋友们欢天喜地，又玩起来了。文彦博灌水得球的故事，一直流传到今天。

## RETRIEVING THE BALL WITH WATER

In the Northern Song Dynasty (960-1127), Wen Yanbo from Jiexiu, Shanxi, was an official for over fifty years and served four emperors at court. He was once promoted to prime minister and later given the title Duke Luguo. He nonetheless often wore simple cotton clothes and drank with his friends, just like any other commoner, and never mentioned his official title. This is a story about an event in his childhood. One day, he was playing ball with his friends, when the ball was kicked into a hole in a tree trunk. One player tried to reach in with his hand to get it out, but it was too far down. Another tried using a stick, but the ball's roundness foiled this method. As everyone was nonplussed, Wen Yanbo came with a basin of water. He poured it into the hole and the ball floated out. All were delighted and started playing again. This story is still passed on today.

## 唐僧取经

是历史上真人真事。公元527-549年，唐太宗年间，僧人玄奘为了研究佛法，孤身一人，到佛教的发祥地天竺国（印度）去取梵文真经。他往返十七年，历经数万里，取得六百多部梵文佛经，运往长安。当时的交通情况，可以想象到路途之艰难。回国后，玄奘口述西行见闻，由他的门徒辩机写成《大唐西域记》。后来，他的门徒慧立、宗惊又写了《大唐大慈恩寺三藏法师传》。随着朝代的更替，唐、宋、元、明，《大唐西域记》也随着朝代而发展。到了明代，江苏淮安吴承恩才写成这部神话故事《西游记》。

## THE TANG PRIEST GOES IN SEARCH OF SCRIPTURES

This is a true story. During the reign of Emperor Tai Zong of the Tang Dynasty (527-549), Priest Xuan Zang went to Tianzhu (today's India), the birthplace of Buddhism, alone to obtain the Sanskrit sutras for the study of Buddhist doctrine. It took him altogether seventeen years to cover a distance of a hundred thousand miles. Eventually he obtained more than six hundred scrolls of sutras in Sanskrit and carried them back to Chang'an, the capital of the Tang. Transportation at that time was very poor and it is not difficult to imagine how difficult travel was for him then. Upon his return, Xuanzang told of what he had seen and heard on his journey to the west to his disciple Bian Ji, who compiled these experiences into a book of Buddhist Records of the Western World in the Tang Dynasty. Later, his disciples Hui Li and Zong Cong wrote another book, The Biography of Master Sanzang of the Great Benevolence Temple of the Great Tang Dynasty. As time went by, the book, Buddhist Records of the Western World in the Tang Dynasty was adapted to the succeeding Tang, Song, Yuan and Ming dynasties. In 1500-1582 of the Ming Dynasty Wu Cheng'en from Huai'an, Jiangsu, finished the mythical story, Journey to the West.

## 举案齐眉

东汉初年，公元25～35年，陕西平陵有个叫梁鸿的隐士，家境一贫如洗，但志向不同常人。他从小勤奋好学，长大博学多才，很多人为他提亲，他都婉言谢绝。平陵孟家有女孟光，面丑体胖，年到三十还没有婆家，声称非梁鸿不嫁。梁鸿听说此事，就娶她为妻，遂入霸陵山隐居，过着男耕女织的惬意生活。他们夫妻恩爱，相敬如宾。每次吃饭，妻子孟光总是将盛饭装菜的托盘高举眉间，请丈夫用饭。"举案齐眉"的典故就是由此而来。

## HOLDING A TRAY AT BROW LEVEL

At the beginning of the Eastern Han Dynasty (25-220), a hermit named Liang Hong lived in Pingling, Shaanxi. His family was very poor, but his ambitions were different from others of his age. During his childhood he was diligent in his studies and fond of learning. When he grew up, he became a learned and versatile man, and many family representatives came to propose marriage to him, but he refused them politely. The Meng family in Pingling had a daughter named Meng Guang who was fat and ugly. At the age of thirty she was still unmarried, and claimed that she would marry no one except Liang Hong. Upon hearing this, Liang Hong took her as his wife and then went into the Baling Mountains to a life of seclusion. They lived a simple but pleasant life, with Liang Hong ploughing the fields and his wife weaving. They loved each other and treated each other with the respect normally only afforded a guest. At each meal Meng Guang would hold a tray filled with rice and dishes up to her brow and present it to her husband for his dinner. The idiom "Holding a tray at brow level" comes from this story.

## 蕉下客

《红楼梦》中第三十七回故事。贾宝玉的三妹探春，住在大观园"秋爽斋"内。一日，月光如洗，她想起姊妹们栖处泉石之间，风庭月榭，帘杏溪桃，又有薛宝钗和林黛玉那么有才气的人。如开吟诗社，也会像古人一样，一时之偶兴，遂成千古之佳谈。便发请帖，请众姊妹来秋爽斋起"海棠诗社"，又为每人起了个别号。黛玉住在潇湘馆，称"潇湘妃子"；宝钗住在蘅芜院，封为"蘅芜君"；宝玉住在怡红院，号称"怡红公子"；探春住处普栽梧桐芭蕉，便叫"蕉下客"。

## THE STRANGER UNDER THE PLANTAIN

This is a story from A Dream of Red Mansions. Jia Baoyu's third sister Tanchun lived at the Studio of Autumn Freshness in the Grand View Garden. One day, the moon looked very clear after the rain, as if it had been washed. The beautiful scenery reminded Tanchun of her sisters living among the fountains and rocks of the garden, and the talented Xue Baochai and Lin Daiyu. She thought it would be fun to organize a poetry club by inviting her sisters and brothers to a feast in a cool courtyard, or a moonlit pavilion, or to compose poetry and drink in the Apricot Tavern by Peach Stream like ancients. She then sent letters to her sisters asking them to gather at the Studio of Autumn Freshness to start the Begonia Club. She also gave everyone a pen name. Daiyu was called Queen of Bamboo, because she lived in Bamboo Lodge; Baochai was called Lady of Alpinia because she lived at the Alpinia Garden; Baoyu was called The Rich and Noble Idler; and Tanchun called herself The Stranger Under the Plantain because her courtyard was planted with Wutong trees and plantains.

## 柴桑口诸葛亮吊丧

赤壁曹操大败，周瑜领兵取南郡，左肋中箭。周瑜诈死，引南郡
兵马来攻，诸葛亮派赵云取了南郡，又以兵符轻取荆州和襄阳。
周瑜气得大叫一声，金疮迸裂。周瑜用计骗刘备去东吴招亲，以
便杀刘备，夺回南郡，又弄拙成真，孙权妹子成了刘备夫人。在
刘备军士大喊声下："周郎妙计安天下，陪了夫人又折兵！"周
瑜金疮再次迸裂。周瑜又用计替刘备取西川，实取荆州，反中了
诸葛亮之计，刘备兵马喊杀震天，又见诸葛亮和刘备在山头悠闲
饮酒，周瑜箭疮复裂而死，年仅三十六岁。诸葛亮又去柴桑口凭
吊周瑜。这是《三国演义》中第五十七回故事。

## ZHUGE LIANG MOURNS ZHOU YU AT CHAISANGKOU

This is a story from Chapter Fifty-Seven of The Three Kingdoms. After Cao Cao was
defeated at the Red Cliff, Zhou Yu took his troops to attack Nanjun, where his chest was
pierced by an arrow, and Zhou Yu pretended to die, thus luring the troops in Nanjun to
launch an attack. Zhuge Liang sent Zhao Yun to capture Nanjun and took over Jingzhou
and Xiangyang easily with a military tally. Zhou Yu was so angry that he cried out and his
wound opened. He concocted a scheme to decoy Liu Bei to the Wu Kingdom to marry
Sun Quan's sister so that he could kill Liu Bei and reclaim Nanjun. The originally false
marriage became real, however, and Sun Quan's sister became Liu Bei's wife. Zhou Yu's
wound again opened as he heard Liu Bei's soldiers shouting: "Young Master Zhou's
brilliant plan of conquest has cost you the lady, and officers and men to boot." Zhou Yu
once again made a plan, ostensibly to capture Xichuan for Liu Bei, but actually to capture
Jingzhou. This time he fell into Zhuge Liang's trap. He heard the shouts of Liu Bei's
soldiers rending the air and saw Zhuge Liang and Liu Bei drinking wine leisurely on the
top of a hill. Zhou Yu's wound opened for the third time and he died at the age of thirty-six.
Zhuge Liang then went to Chaisangkou to offer his condolences to Zhou Yu's family?

## 洛 神

传说上古帝王伏羲的女儿，在洛水堕河身亡，封为洛水女神。中国历代有名的文人都用最美好的词句歌颂洛神的美丽。中国伟大诗人屈原在《离骚》中描写洛神之貌为旷古绝美。公元220～227年，曹操三子曹植才华横溢，下笔成文。有一日他途经洛水驿，梦中得见洛神。曹植为洛神的美貌而倾倒，洛神为曹植的真情而感动，二人倾述了爱慕之情，互赠了礼物。曹植醒来写下文学史上著名的《洛神赋》。中国京戏著名演员梅兰芳主演《洛神》一戏，唱腔优美，久唱不衰。

## THE GODDESS OF LUOSHUI

The Goddess of Luoshui was the daughter of Fu Xi, an ancient emperor of China. She fell into the Luoshui River and drowned, and so became called "the Goddess of Luoshui". Ancient Chinese literary men of all dynasties sang of her beauty in the most refined and flowery manner. Qu Yuan, a great Chinese poet, described her as a lady of matchless beauty from time immemorial. In 220-227, Cao Zhi, the third son of Cao Cao and a literary man of superb talent, went by the Luoshui garrison and saw the goddess in a dream, in which he expressed his admiration for her beauty. The goddess was deeply moved by his sincerity. Both expressed their love for the other and exchanged gifts. On waking up Cao Zhi, wrote "Rhapsody on the Goddess of Luoshui" which became the Peking opera "The Goddess of Luoshui" which Mei Lanfang, the famous Peking Opera actor once performed.

## 富贵寿考

讲的是唐代名将郭子仪从军遇仙的故事。一年，郭子仪奉命催运粮草。他快马加鞭，日夜兼程赶路。一天，途中忽起大风，刮得天昏地暗，他只好躲避。夜里，满天红光驱走了弥漫的沙尘，见五色祥云中，亭亭玉立一位美丽的神仙和随从仙女。原来这一天是七月七日，织女娘娘降世。郭子仪向娘娘跪拜，祈求寿禄，织女娘娘微笑地答应了。后来，河北节度使安禄山和部将史思明叛乱，即中国历史上有名的"安史之乱"，郭子仪率军平定了叛军，保卫了唐王朝，官至极品，福寿双全。

## GUO ZIYI RUNS INTO A FAIRY

One year, Guo Ziyi, a famous general of the Tang Dynasty, received orders to bring an emergency army transport of grains and fodder. He embarked on this journey in all haste, and marched day and night at maximum speed. One day, he was caught in a whirlwind that darkened the sky and obscured everything from view. He had to dismount and find shelter. That night, red lights drove away the dust in the sky to reveal a beautiful fairy standing gracefully on a five-color auspicious cloud with her followers. It was the seventh day of the seventh month that the Goddess of Weaving descended to earth. Guo Ziyi kowtowed to the goddess and prayed for longevity and an official rank. The Goddess of Weaving smiled and accepted his prayers. Later An Lushan and Shi Siming rebelled against the government. Guo Ziyi led troops to put down the rebellious army and safeguarded the Tang court. He was soon promoted to a top official rank and blessed with happiness and longevity.

## 四进士

明代，毛朋、田伦、顾读、刘题四个挚友一起拜户部主事海瑞为师，同时中进士，又同时做京官。他们四人发誓，要像教师那样为官廉正。田伦的姐姐田氏，为霸占家产，毒酒害死小叔子姚廷美，又将姚妻杨素贞卖人。杨素贞发觉，上告到刘题处，刘题上任后嗜酒如命，不理案子。杨素贞告到顾读那里，顾读收到田伦来信和银两，反将杨素贞收监查办。这个案子的来龙去脉，早已被八府巡按毛朋查得一清二楚。他按着四人誓言，惩办了田伦、顾读和刘题。

## FOUR CANDIDATES IN THE HIGHEST OF IMPERIAL EXAMINATIONS

During 1522-1566 of the Ming Dynasty, Mao Peng, Tian Lun, Gu Du and Liu Ti formally became pupils to a master named Hai Rui. They all passed the imperial examinations and worked as officials. They swore to be upright and honest officials like their master. Tian Lun's sister Lady Tian poisoned Yao Tingmei, her husband's brother, and sold Yao's wife Yang Suzhen in order to seize the family's property. Yang Suzhen found out about this, and appealed to a court under the charge of Liu Ti. After Liu Ti had taken office, he often indulged in drinking and neglected his cases. Yang Suzhen went to Gu Du to complain, but Gu Du put Yang Suzhen in prison after receiving a letter and some silver from Tian Lun. Mao Peng had already examined the case thoroughly, and he punished Tian Lun, Gu Du and Liu Ti for violating their oaths.

## 宝玉黛玉读《西厢》

三月中旬一天，宝玉在读《西厢记》。黛玉来到，接过书，不到一顿饭功夫，将十六页俱已看完，却只管出神，心内还默默记诵。宝玉笑道："我就是多愁多病的身，你就是那倾城国倾城的貌。"宝玉把自己和黛玉比做《西厢记》里一对恋人，谈情说爱。黛玉听了不觉带腮连耳通红，薄面含嗔，要去告诉宝玉父母，也就是她的舅舅舅母去，说宝玉把淫词艳曲弄了来欺负她。宝玉着急了，表白说："我若有心欺负你，明天掉在池子里，教瘌头鼋吞了，变个大忘八，等你病老归西的时候，到坟上驮一辈子碑去。"林黛玉这才嗤的一声笑了。这是《红楼梦》第二十三回故事。

## BAOYU AND DAIYU READ THE WESTERN CHAMBER

This is a story from A Dream of Red Mansions. One day in about the middle of the third month, Baoyu was reading The Western Chamber alone in a garden. Daiyu came and took the book from him. In less time than it takes to eat a meal she had finished the sixteen-page book. She then sat there entranced, recalling some of the lines. Baoyu smiled and said to her, "I'm the one 'sick with longing,' and you are the beauty that caused 'cities and kingdoms to fall.'" Baoyu regarded himself and Daiyu as the pair of lovers in The Western Chamber and expressed his love to Daiyu. Daiyu flushed to the tips of her ears. She felt shamed and told Baoyu that she was going to see his parents, her uncle and aunt and tell them Baoyu had insulted her with nasty quotations and licentious songs. In dismay Baoyu said to her, "If I have insulted you, I will jump into the pond tomorrow and have the scabby-headed tortoise swallow me, so that I may turn into a big turtle to bear on my back the stone tablet at your grave when you have grown old and gone at last to your paradise in the west." Lin Daiyu burst out laughing at his words.

## 猛张飞智取瓦口关

《三国演义》中第七十回故事。张飞和魏延连日攻打瓦口关不下。张飞见不济事，把军退二十里，却和魏延引数十骑，来关外两边哨探小路。忽见男女数人，于山僻路攀藤附葛而走。张飞便把他们带回寨中，给予酒食。张飞由他们带路，绕道插于瓦口关背后，命魏延引兵正面攻打瓦口关。守关将领张郃正要下山，忽报关后四、五路火起。张郃领兵来迎，见是张飞，大吃一惊，弃了瓦口关，寻径而逃。猛张飞用智夺得瓦口关，为刘备取汉中立下功劳。

## FIERCE ZHANG FEI TAKES
## THE WAKOU PASS BY STRATEGY

This is a story from The Three Kingdoms. Zhang Fei and Wei Yan attacked the Wakou Pass for several days, but failed to take it, and so gave up and retreated ten kilometers. On leading a dozen soldiers to scout the surrounding paths, they discovered some men and women clambering along the hill by clutching vines. Zhang Fei ordered his men to bring them to the camp and treat them with wine and food. Then he asked them to lead the way and went around to the back of the Wakou Pass, while making Wei Yan lead a frontal attack. The general of the pass, Zhang He, was about to go down the hill when it was reported to him that there were fires in four or five places behind the pass. He immediately took his soldiers there and was startled to see Zhang Fei. He turned his horse around and escaped. Zhang Fei's success at the pass helped Liu Bei to overtake Hangzhong.

## 晴雯病补孔雀裘

《红楼梦》中第五十二回故事。贾宝玉房内丫鬟晴雯生得美丽，事事要强，这几日伤风咳嗽。掌灯时分，宝玉回房，进门就口嘻声跺脚。原来白日贾母给宝玉一件用孔雀毛拈了线织的"雀金"披裘，被宝玉不小心烧了一块。丫鬟急派婆子出去修补，结果甭说织补匠人，就是裁缝绣匠都不认识这是什么衣服。晴雯说："说不得，我挣命罢了。"她一面说，一面坐起来，只觉头重身轻，满眼金星乱迸，补上三五针，伏在枕上歇一会，只听自鸣钟敲了四下，刚刚补完，又用小牙刷慢慢地剔出绒毛来，嗳哟一声，便身不由主倒下了。

## PLUCKY QINGWEN MENDS A PEACOCK FEATHER CAPE IN BED

This is a story from A Dream of Red Mansions. Qingwen, one of Baoyu's maids, was very pretty and eager to excel. She had recently caught a cold and had a bad cough. At lighting up time Baoyu returned, sighing and stamping his feet. That morning Baoyu's grandmother had given Baoyu a peacock-feather cape called "golden peacock felt." Unfortunately he had accidentally burned a hole in it. His maid hurriedly sent an older servant out to have it patched, but the woman returned and said that no weavers, or tailors, or embroiderers knew what that cape was. Qingwen said: "There's nothing else for it then but to try my best." With that she sat up feeling so dizzy that stars danced before her eyes. After a couple of stitches she stopped and rested on her pillow for a while, and finished mending the cape just as the clock struck four. She then fluffed up the down with a small toothbrush and sank back in bed with a groan.

## 唐玄宗夜游月宫

公元712-742年，有个叫罗公远的道士，道术出神入化，被召进宫中，伴君解闷。这年八月中秋夜晚，皓月当空，罗公远陪伴玄宗在御花园中赏月。罗公远提出带玄宗到月亮里玩玩。只见道士将拂尘往空中一掷，拂尘变成一座彩桥。道士扶着玄宗上桥，那桥便直上九霄，来到月宫。嫦娥引众仙女出来迎人间皇帝，仙娥献上桂花美酒。仙乐奏起，众仙女翩翩起舞。唐玄宗从未听过这样动人的乐曲，从未看过这样美妙绝伦的舞姿。这就是《霓裳羽衣曲》，唐玄宗带回人间。盛唐歌舞在中国历朝为先，此曲舞在唐代为最，一直流传到今天。

## EMPEROR XUAN ZONG OF TANG VISITS THE MOON PALACE AT NIGHT

In 712-742 a Taoist priest named Luo Gongyuan whose Taoist skills were superb, was called to the palace. He was asked to keep the emperor company and divert him from boredom. In the evening of the Mid-Autumn Festival on the eighth month of that year, the moon was bright in the sky. Luo Gongyuan accompanied the emperor Xuan Zong to enjoy the view of the beautiful full moon in the imperial garden. Luo Gongyuan suggested taking Xuan Zong to the moon. As he spoke, he threw dust into the sky that turned into a rainbow bridge. The Taoist priest held the emperor's arm as they crossed the bridge up to heaven. When they arrived at the Moon Palace, Chang'e, along with other celestials, came to greet the emperor and presented him with wine fermented with osmanthus flowers. Celestial music played and all the celestials started to dance. Emperor Xuan Zong had never heard such enchanting music, nor seen such wonderful dancing. It was the "Music of the Rainbow and Feathery Garments", well-known dance music, brought back to the world from heaven by Xuan Zong of Tang. Singing and dancing in China originated at the zenith of the Tang Dynasty. This dancing music was the most famous of the Tang Dynasty and has been passed on till today.

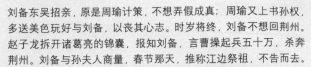

## 刘备智激孙夫人

刘备东吴招亲，原是周瑜计策，不想弄假成真；周瑜又上书孙权，多送美色玩好与刘备，以丧其心志。时岁将终，刘备不想回荆州。赵子龙拆开诸葛亮的锦囊，报知刘备，言曹操起兵五十万，杀奔荆州。刘备与孙夫人商量，春节那天，推称江边祭祖，不告而去。

## LIU BEI WINS OVER LADY SUN WITH STRATEGY

This is a story from The Three Kingdoms. Liu Bei went to the Wu Kingdom for a proposed marriage that was actually a scheme of Zhou Yu, but which in the end became reality. Zhou Yu therefore sent in a memorial to Sun Quan. He suggested they presented more beautiful girls and entertainment to Liu Bei in order to sap his will to make progress. As the year came to its close, Liu Bei indulged in an easy life in the Wu Kingdom and did not want to return to Jingzhou. Zhao Zilong opened a brocade bag from which he took out and read a report to Liu Bei that Cao Cao was heading for Jingzhou with 500,000 troops. Liu Bei planned with Lady Sun that they should leave without saying

这日孙权大醉，第二天五更方醒，得知走了刘备，派大将陈武、潘璋追赶。刘备正行，见后面追兵到来，前面大将徐盛、丁奉引三千兵马，奉周瑜之命截击，赵云拆开军师锦囊，是求孙夫人。孙夫人出面，骂得四员大将面面相觑，只好放行。诸葛亮亲领大船，接回刘备。这是《三国演义》中第五十五回故事。

goodbye on the Chinese New Year's day with the excuse that they were going to the river bank to pay respects to their ancestors. That day, Sun Quan was completely drunk and did not wake up till the following morning. Having heard that Liu Bei had already left, he immediately dispatched generals Chen Wu and Pan Zhang to pursue them. As Liu Bei rushed on, he saw soldiers coming up behind, and Xu Sheng and Ding Feng with three thousand men blocking the road ahead of them under the orders of Zhou Yu. Zhao Zilong opened the third brocade bag prepared by Zhuge Liang. In it was a report advising them to seek help from Lady Sun. Lady Sun approached the four generals and upbraided them. The four generals looked at each other and had to let Lady Sun's party pass. Zhuge Liang came himself with a boat and brought Liu Bei back to Jingzhou.

## 苏小妹三难新郎

《醒世恒言》中故事。宋代大文豪苏东坡的妹妹苏小妹，从小聪颖过人，长大满腹经纶，不让须眉，要选天下才子匹配。凡是求婚者，均送上一篇文章，由小妹自己批点择婿。落选者不计其数。扬州秀才秦少游，投文求婚，被苏小妹选中。成婚那天，恰是少游金榜高中之日，真是"洞房花烛夜，金榜题名时"。这一夜月

## SU XIAOMEI POSES THREE QUESTIONS TO HER BRIDEGROOM

This is a story from Xingshihengyan. Su Xiaomei, the younger sister of Su Dongpo, a great literary man of the Song Dynasty, had been exceptionally bright ever since her childhood. When she grew up, she became a lady of superb knowledge who did not defer to men. She determined to marry a talented man. All who proposed marriage to her had to submit an essay for her evaluation. Many failed this selection process. The scholar Qin Shaoyou from Yangzhou also submitted an essay and was selected by Su Xiaomei. As chance would have it, their wedding day fell on the day that Qin Shaoyou was informed that he had passed the highest imperial examination. Alas, as the

儿皎洁，洞房却紧闭。房外八仙桌上放着苏小妹出的三个题目。新郎先解题，后入洞房。第一题是一句绝句，第二题是猜谜，少游提笔一挥而就。第三题是对句，只见上句写道："闲门推出窗前月"，少游一时想不出好句，嘴里念念有词，绕着花缸走来走去。苏东坡一觉醒来，拣小石投向缸中，少游顿开茅塞，写出："投石冲开水底天"。苏小妹三难新郎，苏东坡投石成全的故事还编成各种剧目。

saying goes, "a wedding night comes along with success in the imperial examination." That night the moon was very bright, but the door of the bridal chamber was tightly shut. Three questions written by Su Xiaomei were laid on a table. The bridegroom had to answer all of them before entering the bridal chamber. The first question was a quatrain and the second was a riddle that was easily solved by Qin Shaoyou. The third test was to compose a line in antiphonal style. The first line written by Su Xiaomei was: "An idle door pushed away(open) the moon from in front of the window." Qin Shaoyou could not at first find the right words. He mumbled, and paced back and forth around a flower vat. When Su Dongpo woke up from a sleep, he picked up a pebble, threw it into the vat and Qin Shaoyou suddenly saw the light. He at once wrote: "A thrown pebble broke apart the sky at the bottom of the water." This story has made into many different plays and operas.

 烟霞天成

 184

## 杨排风单骑战殷奇

《杨家将》中的故事。公元1100年，宋朝国势衰弱，西夏国派元帅殷奇领兵进犯中原。宋军屡战屡败，边关告急，朝内无将御敌。穆桂英以国家为重，再次挂帅征西，命杨排风为先锋。这杨排风本是杨家烧火丫头，但胸怀大志，烧火之余，苦练武艺，在杨家崭露头角。穆桂英领兵西来，先埋伏杨排风一支兵马，再与西夏兵马交锋。两军对阵，宋军大败。那殷奇司空见惯，亲自率军追杀。他正在追赶，路旁林中杀出一支人马，白马银枪杨排风直取殷奇。只十几个回合，殷奇招架不住，落荒逃走，杨家军乘势掩杀过去，西夏军大败而逃。

## YANG PAIFENG'S COMBAT WITH YIN QI

This is a story from Generals of the Yang Family. In 1100 the Song court was in decline. The Xixia State sent general Yin Qi with its troops to invade the Central Plains. The Song army was repeatedly defeated. The frontier passes frantically signaled for emergency help, but the court could find no generals to defend it against the enemy. For the sake of the country, Mu Guiying once more took command of an expedition westward against the Xixia troops, and ordered Yang Paifeng to be the vanguard. Yang Paifeng was only a kitchen maid, but she had practiced martial arts very hard in her spare time and displayed remarkable talent. Mu Guiying led the army westward. She first made Yang Paifeng take a small number of soldiers to stage an ambush in a forest, and then fought the Xixia troops. When the two sides met, the Song troops feigned retreat. Yin Qi knew this strategy and led his troops in pursuit. Suddenly a group of soldiers led by Yang Paifeng riding on her white horse grasping a silver spear appeared from the forest and charged Yin Qi. After only a dozen rounds Yin Qi was unable to withstand this attack and fled. The Yang family troops pressed their advantage and fought their way on. The Xixia troops suffered a crushing defeat and fled back to their country.

## 鱼肠剑

春秋战国时期，公元前527年，公子僚取得吴国王位。本来继承王位的公子光，心怀仇恨，发誓夺回王位。公子光结识勇士专诸，视如亲人，待遇甚厚。专诸过意不去，表示说："只要公子有用我之处，万死不辞。"公子光说了吴王僚夺位之仇。还告诉专诸吴王喜欢吃鱼。专诸拜名师学烧鱼三月有余。一日，公子光宴请吴王。吴王怕人行刺，内穿名贵铠甲防身，外派卫兵搜查每个厨师全身。专诸端上一条红烧糖醋鲤鱼，远远香气扑鼻。吴王站起来连声说："好！好！"专诸端鱼在吴王前敬献，吴王正在高兴，专诸拔出鱼身内藏的短剑，刺向吴王胸膛，那剑直透铠甲，吴王大叫一声，当场毙命。"鱼肠剑"由此得名。

## FISH INTESTINE DAGGER

In 527 BC, during the Spring and Autumn Period, Prince Liao ascended the Wu State throne. Prince Guang, the original successor to the throne, felt bitter hatred towards Prince Liao and swore to seize back the throne. Prince Guang met a brave man named Zhuan Zhu whom he came to regard as his own brother and treated very well. Zhuan Zhu felt guilty about this and said to Prince Guang, "I'm willing to die for my prince as long as you need me." Prince Guang then expressed his hatred for King Liao of Wu and told him that the King of Wu liked to eat fish. Zhuan Zhu spent more than three months learning how to cook fish from a master. One day, Prince Guang invited the King of Wu to a feast. The King of Wu was afraid of being assassinated so he wore precious armor inside his clothes and ordered his guards to make a body search of every cook. Zhuan Zhu brought up a dish of stewed, sweet and sour carp that emitted a delicious aroma. The King of Wu stood up and said again and again, "Excellent, excellent!" Zhuan Zhu held up the fish and presented it to the king. As the king was consumed with delight, Zhuan Zhu suddenly pulled out a dagger hidden inside the fish and stabbed the king in the heart. The dagger pierced the armor and found its target. The King of Wu gave a cry and died on spot. This is how the "fish intestine dagger" got its name.

## 八仙过海

八仙乃是铁拐李、汉钟离、蓝采和、吕洞宾、张果老、韩湘子、何仙姑、曹国舅。他们每人都有一段成仙经历，在中国广泛流传。图中讲的是八神结伴东游，乘船过东海的故事，只是传说之一。其实八仙过海，都以各人的神通渡过，否则中国成语就不会留下＂八仙过海，各显神通＂之说了。

## THE EIGHT IMMORTALS CROSS THE SEA

The eight immortals were Tieguai Li, Han Zhongli, Lan Caihe, Lü Dongbin, Zhang Guolao, Han Xiangzi, He Xiangu, and Cao Guojiu. Each of them had a story of how they become immortal. This story is very popular in China. This painting tells the story of the eight immortals crossing the Eastern Sea together by boat, and is only one of the legends about them. Each immortal had his own special prowess through which to cross the ocean, otherwise they would not have left us with this famous Chinese proverb: "The eight immortals cross the sea, each one shows his or her special prowess."

## 据汉水赵子龙以寡胜众

曹操自领大军二十万，兵发汉中。老将黄忠和赵子龙同往，烧曹兵粮草。赵子龙在汉水边安营扎寨，黄忠和副将张著偷过汉水，直到北山，见粮积如山，正欲放火，魏将张郃、徐晃兵到，将黄忠困在垓心；魏将文聘又将张著围住。赵子龙在营中等到午时，不见黄忠回，遂引三千军接应。赵子龙连杀两员魏将，见张郃、徐晃两人围住黄忠，大喝一声，枪舞梨花，救出黄忠。子龙所到之处，无人敢阻，又救出张著，直透重围，过汉水回寨。这是《三国演义》中第七十一回故事。

## ZHAO ZILONG'S FEW OVERCOME MANY BY THE HANSHUI RIVER

This is a story from The Three Kingdoms. Cao Cao led 200,000 troops in an attack on Hanzhong. The old general Huang Zhong and Zhao Zilong went together to burn Cao's troops' store of grain. Zhao Zilong camped on the Hanshui river bank, while Huang Zhong and his lieutenant Zhang Zhu stealthily crossed Hanshui River and reached the Northern Mountain, where they saw a pile of grain the size of a hill. They were about to set fire to it when Cao's troops, led by Zhang He and Xu Huang, arrived and surrounded Huang Zhong, while another general, Wen Pin, encircled Zhang Zhu. Zhao Zilong waited at his camp till noon, but, seeing that Huang Zhong was not going to return, took 3,000 soldiers to aid Huang Zhong and Zhang Zhu. Zhao Zilong slayed the two Wei generals one after another. Seeing Huang Zhong had been intercepted by Zhang He and Xu Huang, Zhao Zilong cried out and brandished his spear as he charged and went to aid Huang Zhong. Zhao Zilong's spear work was so deadly skillful that no one dared to stop him. Zhao Zilong finally rescued Zhang Zhu, broke through the encirclement, and returned to camp.

## 讳疾忌医

《史记·扁鹊传》中记载。战国时期，名医扁鹊见齐桓公，言他有病，病在皮肤里。齐桓公不高兴地说："我没有病。"又过五天，扁鹊见齐桓公，又告之，病已入血脉，齐桓公还是不信。又过五天，扁鹊见齐桓公，告知病已入肠胃，齐桓公置之不理。又过五天，扁鹊来见齐桓公，一见面，转身就走。齐桓公派人去问究竟。扁鹊说："病在皮肤，可用药敷；病在血脉，可用针灸；病入肠胃，可用汤药；现在病入骨髓，没有办法了。五天后，齐桓公一病不起，扁鹊不知去向，齐桓公病死了。

## AVOID SEEING A DOCTOR OUT OF RESENTMENT FOR ILLNESS

According to the Biography of Bian Que in the Historical Records, during the Warring States Period (475-221BC) a famous doctor named Bian Que went to see Qi Henggong, emperor of the State of Qi one day. He told the emperor that he was sick, but that the disease only affected his skin. Qi Henggong said unhappily, "I'm all right." Five days later, Bian Que met Qi again and told him that the disease had entered his blood vessels. Qi did not believe him. After another five days, Bian Que met Qi and warned him that the disease had attacked the stomach. Qi Henggong still paid no attention to his words. Five more days went by, and Bian Que went to visit Qi Henggong. As soon as Bian Que set eyes on Qi, he quickly turned around and left. Qi sent someone to ask Bian Que the reason. Bian Que said: "If the skin is affected, it can be dressed with ointment; if the disease is in the blood vessels, acupuncture can be used; if the disease goes to the stomach, medical herbs can be applied; now the disease has attacked the marrow and there is no way to deal with it. Five days later, Qi Henggong fell ill and lay in bed. Bian Que had already left without any trace. Soon, Qi Henggong died of illness.

## 老鹰抓小鸡

中国古代流传下来的一种儿童游戏。小鸡由数个小孩组成，摆开一字长蛇。鸡头一动牵动鸡身、鸡尾。只有动作一致，整齐划一，才能有效地躲闪老鹰扑捉。许多人曾伴随它度过童年。

## AN EAGLE CATCHES CHICKS

This is a traditional Chinese game for children. Usually several children pretend to be chicks and line up, each holding on to the backs of the one before them. When the first child as the head of the chicks moves, the rest at the back imitate his/her movements. As long as they all act in the same way and move in the same direction, they can dodge effectively and avoid being caught by the eagle.

## 文王访贤

前面讲过姜太公钓鱼。商朝末期，纣王荒淫残暴，朝廷腐败，民不聊生。渭水流域周国姬昌要救民于水火之中，广召天下英雄，要灭商兴周。姬昌听说渭水磻溪河边，有一老人用无饵直钩钓鱼，意不在鱼，而在圣君，便亲自来访。此时，姜子牙已年近八旬，姬昌有问必答，使姬昌心悦诚服，遂接姜子牙回城。姬昌就是后来的周文王。姜子牙又挂帅兴兵伐纣，帮助文王儿子周武王推翻了商朝，建立了周朝。

## KING WEN VISITS THE SAGE

Towards the end of the Shang Dynasty, King Zhou's behavior was crude and licentious. The court was corrupt, and the people lived in dire poverty. Jichang, from the State of Zhou, on the reaches of the Wei River, determined to liberate the people from their misery. He summoned all the heroes under heaven with the intention of overthrowing the Shang Dynasty and establishing the Zhou Dynasty. When Jichang heard of an old man that stood on the bank of the Pan tributary of the Wei River, and fished with a straight hook, without bait, and whose aim was not to catch fish, but a wise ruler, he decided to go and to see him. At this time Jiang Ziya [the old man] was nearly eighty years old. He answered all the questions raised by Jichang, who was completely convinced of his wisdom, and took Jiang Ziya back with him to the city. Jichang later became King Wen of the Zhou Dynasty. Jiang Ziya subsequently took command and sent a punitive expedition against King Zhou. He eventually helped King Wu, son of King Wen, to overthrow the Shang Dynasty and establish the Zhou Dynasty.

## "功名未必胜鲈鱼"

这是宋代诗人表达晋朝张翰为人的诗句。晋时，苏州人张翰在朝为官，见到官场黑暗，战祸连年，想起家乡的鲈鱼片，感慨人生，何必违背自己的意愿，为名利而远离家乡在外为官呢？遂起退隐之念。张翰归乡后随心所欲，或开怀饮酒，或挥毫撰文，或游历名山大川，自由自在，无拘无束。张翰行为引起无数文人的称道，但真正舍得放弃名利回乡吃鲈鱼片的，却没有几个人。

## AN OFFICIAL RANK IS PERHAPS NO BETTER THAN A PERCH

This is a poem written by a poet of the Song Dynasty to express the integrity of Zhang Han of the Jin Dynasty. During the Jin Dynasty (265-317), Zhang Han from Suzhou served as an official at court. Seeing the corruption of official circles and unceasing disasters of war year after year, he remembered the perch slices in his hometown. He sighed with emotion for a man's life - why should a man leave his hometown against his will to seek an official rank and work as an official elsewhere? Then he suddenly felt the impulse to resign. After returning home, Zhang Han did whatever he liked, sometimes drank to his content, sometimes wrote articles, or traveled all over the country to visit famous mountains and rivers. He was totally unconstrained, as free as a bird. Zhang Han's behavior was praised by many literary men, however very few people were willing to give up an official rank to return to their hometown to eat a perch slice.

## 东山丝竹

东晋谢安，做官前曾在东山隐居，整日同朋友游玩在林泉之间。他命从人携带笛、箫、笙、二胡、琵琶等乐器，走到哪里就在哪里吹、拉、弹、奏，好不惬意。"东山丝竹"由此得名。后来，谢安四十岁的时候应召出山，在朝从政。到公元373年，官拜宰相，成为东晋时著名的政治家。

## STRINGED AND WOODWIND INSTRUMENTS OF THE EASTERN HILLS

Xie An of the Eastern Jin Dynasty lived in seclusion in the Eastern Hills before becoming an official. He spent all day with his friends enjoying the woods and springs, and would ask his friends to bring a flute, a vertical bamboo flute, a sheng (a reed pipe wind instrument), an erhu (a two-stringed instrument), a sanxian (a three-stringed plucked instrument) and a pipa (a plucked string instrument with a fretted fingerboard). Wherever they went, they joyfully played their instruments. "Stringed and Woodwind Instruments of the Eastern Hill" was thus named. Later, when Xie An was in his forties, he was called to serve at court. In 373, he was promoted to prime minister and became a well-known politician of the Eastern Jin Dynasty.

## 劈山救母

中国神话故事。书生刘彦昌进京赶考，途经华山，拜三圣母祠。他见三圣母像端庄美丽，便写下爱慕的诗句。三圣母得知，私自下凡与刘彦昌结为夫妻，并生下儿子，取名沉香。三圣母哥哥二郎神将妹妹压在华山脚下惩罚。婴儿沉香的啼哭声惊动了霹雳大仙，大仙抱回婴儿，收养为徒。十五年后，大仙交沉香一把开山神斧，叫他救母。沉香打败了舅舅二郎神，劈开华山，救出母亲，又找到失散的父亲。劈山救母的故事编成戏剧、舞剧，深受百姓欢迎。

## SPLITTING THE MOUNTAIN TO RESCUE HIS MOTHER

This is a Chinese folktale. The scholar Liu Yanchang went to the capital city to take the imperial examination. Going by way of Mount Hua, he went to worship the Third Holy Mother at a temple. He was so impressed by the beauty and dignity of the statue of the Third Holy Mother that he wrote a poem to express his love for her. When the Third Holy Mother heard, she stealthily descended to earth and married Liu Yanchang bearing him a son named Chen Xiang. The Third Holy Mother's brother, God Erlang, punished his sister by placing her beneath Mount Hua. The cries of the baby Chen Xiang woke the Thunderbolt God. He carried the baby home and took him as his disciple. Fifteen years later, he handed Chen Xiang a magic axe and told him to rescue his mother. Chen Xiang defeated his uncle, the God of Erlang, and rescued his mother by splitting Mount Hua, and also found his long lost father. This story has been adapted into dramas and dances, and is very popular among the Chinese people.

## 蒋干盗书

曹操亲领百万大军要灭东吴，周瑜率战船先胜曹操一阵，次日又单船窥探曹营水寨。曹操问手下当作何计破之。帐下谋士蒋干是周瑜幼年同窗，愿说周瑜来降。蒋干来东吴，周瑜整衣冠，引从者数百人迎之，又大张筵席，轮换行酒，接待蒋干。当夜，周瑜与蒋干抵足而眠。瑜佯作大醉，呕吐狼藉。鼓打二更，瑜鼻息如雷。蒋干见桌上堆着文件，起床偷视之，内有一封上写蔡瑁张允谨封。遂将书暗藏于衣内，潜步出帐，飞棹回见曹操。曹操见信大怒，立斩蔡帽、张允，方省悟中计。那蔡、张为水军都督，深得水军之妙，是周瑜心头人患。

## JIANG GAN STEALS A LETTER

Cao Cao led his million troops in a campaign to wipe out the Wu Kingdom. Zhou Yu commanded his warships and won the first battle against Cao Cao. The next day, Zhou Yu sent a boat to gather intelligence about Cao Cao's water camp, and Cao Cao asked his subordinates to deal with the matter. Jiang Gan, one of Cao Cao's military advisers, had been Zhou Yu's classmate and volunteered to persuade Zhou Yu to surrender. When Jiang Gan arrived at Wu Kingdom, Zhou Yu dressed in his finest, and led a hundred of his subordinates to greet him. He then laid a grand banquet for him. Zhou Yu and his men took turns toasting Jiang Gan and treated him warmly. That night Zhou Yu slept together with Jiang Gan in the same tent. Zhou Yu pretended to be completely drunk and vomited all the food he had eaten. At the second watch, Zhou Yu's snores were like thunder. Having spied a pile of documents on the table Jiang Gan got up and thumbed through them stealthily. Among the documents was a letter from Cai Mao and Zhang Yun urging Zhou Yu to surrender. Jiang Gan stuffed it inside his tunic, tiptoed out of the tent and swiftly returned to Cao's camp. Cao Cao was enraged after reading this letter and immediately had Cai Mao and Zhang Yun executed. He later realized that he had played right into Zhou Yu's hands, as the navy generals Cai Mao and Zhang Yun knew the arts of naval war very well, and had become Zhou Yu's biggest worry.

## 李逵大闹忠义堂

梁山泊好汉李逵和燕青在刘太公庄上投宿,听太公太婆哭了一夜,天明得知宋江把他家女儿抢走。李逵回到梁山忠义堂,睁圆怪眼,拔出大斧,砍掉了"替天行道"的杏黄旗。宋江同李逵来到庄上对质,李逵才知有人冒宋江名做坏事。李逵自把衣服脱了,将麻绳绑缚了,脊梁上背着一把荆杖,向宋江负荆请罪。宋江道:"若要我饶你,只教你捉得那两个假宋江。"数日后,李逵救出刘太公女儿,带着两个假宋江人头,驮着两贼的数千两金银回山交令。这是《水浒传》中第七十三回故事。

## LI KUI STIRS UP TROUBLE AT LOYALTY HALL

This is a story from Outlaws of the Marsh. Li Kui and Yan Qing, two heroes from Mount Liang, spent a night at the squire Liu's manor. They heard the squire's wife crying the whole night, and heard the next morning that her daughter had been kidnapped by Song Jiang. After Li Kui returned to Mount Liang, he went directly to Loyalty Hall. His eyes glaring in anger, he took his axes out and cut down the apricot-yellow banner inscribed with "Act in Heaven's Behalf". Later Song Jiang and Li Kui went to the manor and confronted the squire. It was then that Li Kui discovered that someone else had committed this crime in Song Jiang's name. Li Kui took off his clothes, had himself tied up, placed a briar on his bare back and asked Song Jiang to beat him with it for his mistake. Song Jiang said: "I'll forgive you if you capture the two impersonators." Several days later, Li Kui rescued the squire's daughter and went back to Mount Liang carrying the two heads of the impersonators and a thousand pieces of silver and gold that he had taken from the two chieftains.

## 黄英

《聊斋志异》中故事。以前有个叫马子才的人，喜爱菊花。一日，他从金陵买菊回来，路遇一姓陶的英俊少年，言谈高雅，深得养菊之法。子才大喜，邀请少年和少年姐姐到家里来住。少年将马子才所弃的残枝劣种菊花全部拾起，种在南院。没几天，菊花开，其花皆异种，目所未睹。不久，子才妻子病故。子才向少年的姐姐黄英求婚，黄英答应下来。陶家弟弟豪饮，一日，饮过百壶，变成了菊花，黄英抢救及时，又变回人形。马子才这才知道姐弟是菊精，心中更是高兴。又一次陶弟酒醉变成菊花而死。其姐黄英将一段根栽在盆中，浇酒则茂，花开散发酒香，名为"醉陶"。

## HUANG YING

This is a story from Strange Tales from the Make-Do Studio. Ma Zicai was fond of chrysanthemums. One day, he went to Jinling (today's Nanjing) to buy flowers. On his way back he met a handsome young man surnamed Tao, who talked in an elegant way and had a profound knowledge of chrysanthemum cultivation. Zicai was very pleased and invited the young man and his sister, Huang Ying, to his home. The young man picked up all the withered branches of the chrysanthemum Zicai had discarded and planted them in the south courtyard. A few days later, all the branches had bloomed and the flowers changed into varieties no one had ever seen. Before long, Zicai's wife died of illness and Zicai proposed a marriage to Tao's sister, Huang Ying, who accepted. Huang Ying's brother liked drinking. One day, after he had drunk a hundred pots of wine he turned into a chrysanthemum. Luckily Huang Ying rescued him in time and made him change back to human form. It was only then that Ma Zicai realized that the young man and his sister Huang Ying were chrysanthemum spirits. Huang Ying planted a length of root in a flowerpot. It soon grew luxuriantly and when in bloom emitted the fragance of wine. Hence this species was called "Drunken Tao".

## 麒麟献书

麒麟是中国古代传说中的一种动物，金身鳞甲，金光闪闪，头如鹿，尾如牛，却非牛非鹿，非凡间动物。它能给人带来祥瑞，因此在故宫、颐和园里都有摆放。传说春秋时代的孔子，就是麒麟受天帝之命，献书与他，使他成为中国圣人。

## THE KYLIN PRESENTS BOOKS

The kylin is a mythical animal in China. It is golden, with shining scales, and has the head of a deer and the tail of an ox. It brings good luck, and its bronze image stands before the Forbidden City and the Summer Palace. It is said that in 476 BC during the Spring and Autumn Period, the kylin presented three precious books to Confucius, by order of the Emperor of Heaven, thus making him the sage of China.

## 撕扇作千金一笑

这年端阳佳节之筵，大家无兴散了，宝玉长吁短叹回房。偏生晴雯上来换衣服，又把扇股跌折。宝玉叹道："蠢才，蠢才！"晴雯嘴不让人，气的宝玉浑身乱战。袭人来劝，晴雯又括上袭人。宝玉外出吃酒，晚间回来，晴雯还在生气。宝玉说："那扇子你要撕着玩也可以，不要生气时拿他出气。这就是爱物了。"晴雯说："我最喜欢撕扇子。"宝玉递与她扇子，晴雯接过来，嗤的一声，撕了两半。接着又连着撕扇子，二人大笑。宝玉笑道："千金难买美人笑，几把扇子能值几何！"这是《红楼梦》中第三十一回故事。

## A TORN FAN WINS A SMILE FROM A MAID

This is a story from A Dream of Red Mansions. When the party for the Double Fifth Festival ended, all the guests departed. Baoyu went back to his room feeling so gloomy that he did nothing but sighed. At this moment, as Qingwen helped him change clothes, she dropped his fan and broke it. "How stupid you are!" exclaimed Baoyu. Qingwen was not the kind of maid who took kindly to being scolded. She retorted and made Baoyu tremble with rage. Xiren hurried in and tried to stop her, but was dragged into trouble by Qingwen. Baoyu then left for a drinking party. When he returned that evening, he found that Qingwen was still angry. So he said to her, "You can tear it if you want. But you shouldn't vent your anger on it when you are unhappy. That's what's called caring for things." Qingwen said: "I love tearing up fans." Baoyu handed her a fan that she immediately ripped in two. Qingwen tore up several more fans and both of them laughed. Then Baoyu said: "A thousand pieces of gold can hardly purchase a smile. What are a few fans worth?"

## 诉肺腑心迷活宝玉

贾宝玉只知在女人堆里搅，那宝钗讲些仕途学问，他认为是混帐话，认黛玉为知己。黛玉听了又喜又惊，又悲又叹。宝玉出屋见黛玉在前面边走边拭泪，赶上说："难道我素日在你身上的心都用错了？连你的意思若体贴不着，就难怪你天天为我生气了。"接着又说："你皆因总是不放心的原故，才弄了一身病。但凡宽慰些，这病也不得一日重似一日。"林黛玉听了这话，如轰雷掣电，细细思之，竟比自己肺腑中掏出来的还恳切，两眼不觉滚下泪来。黛玉走了，宝玉只管发起呆来。这是《红楼梦》中第三十三回故事。

## AN AVOWAL LEAVES BAOYU BEMUSED

This is a story from A Dream of Red Mansions. Jia Baoyu grew up among women. He thought what Baochai said about the knowledge required for an official career was nonsense and considered Daiyu as his intimate friend. Daiyu was pleasantly surprised yet sighed mournfully to hear this. Baoyu saw Daiyu walking ahead wiping her tears and caught up with her saying: "Could it be that since I've known you all my feelings for you have been wrong? If I can't even enter into your feelings, then you're quite right to be angry with me all the time." He continued, "You ruin your health by worrying so much. If you'd take things less to heart, your illness wouldn't be getting worse every day." These words struck Daiyu like a thunderbolt. As she turned them over in her mind, they seemed closer to her innermost thoughts than if wrung from her own heart. Tears streamed down her cheeks. Daiyu hurried off leaving Baoyu standing there as if in a trance.

## 《独鹤吟》

唐代诗人李咸诗。李咸颇有才气，但科举不中，仕途无门，却恨起平庸无能之辈混入官场了。他把自己比作孤独的仙鹤，直飞轻上九重天，逍遥自在，不再与尘世有染。全诗如下：

　　"碧玉喙长丹顶圆，亭亭危立风松间。
　　啄萍吞鳞意已阑，举头咫尺轻重天。
　　黑翎白本排云烟，离群脱侣孤如仙。
　　披霜泪月惊婵娟，逍遥忘却还青田。
　　鸢寒鸦晚空相喧，时时侧耳清冷泉。"

## SONG OF A LONELY CRANE

This is a poem written by Li Xian of the Tang Dynasty. Li Xian had enormous talent, but failed to pass the imperial examinations, and had no way of achieving an official rank. He hated the kind of mediocre people who wormed their way into official circles. He regarded himself as a lonely crane which flew straight to heaven, free and unfettered, and had no ties with the world. The poem reads:

　　Pure white body with a long beak and a red crown,
　　I stand elegantly in the wind among the pines.
　　I leisurely peck the grass and eat fish,
　　Raising my head I fly to heaven.
　　Black feathered birds line up like a cloud,
　　Leaving the flock and my partner, I become solitary like an immortal.
　　Leisurely and carefree I forget to return to the green field.
　　Crows cry in vain in the evening sky,
　　While I listen to the bubbling of pure, cold, springs.

## 香菱斗草

贾宝玉、平儿、薛宝琴、邢岫烟同一天过生日，大观园内好不热闹。香菱、芳官、蕊官、藕官、豆官五人，满园中顽了一回，每人又采了花草，坐在一起斗草。这一个说："我有观音柳。"那一个说："我有罗汉松。"那一个又说："我有君子竹。"这一个又说："我有美人蕉。"这个又说："我有星星翠。"那个又说："我有月月红。"豆官说："我有姐妹花。"众人对不上，香菱便说："我有夫妻蕙。"豆官不服，便争论、打闹起来。这是《红楼梦》中第六十二回故事。

## XIANGLING PLAYS WITH TWIGS

This is a story from A Dream of Red Mansions. It was a very lively time in the Grand View Garden because Jia Baoyu, Ping'er, Xue Baoqin, and Xing Youyuan all celebrated their birthdays on the same day. Xiangling, Fangguan, Ruiguan, Ouguan and Douguan played a game in the garden. They each picked a twig and had a competition as to whose was the best. One of them said: "I've got a Guanyin willow." Another said: "I've got a yew podocarpus." Someone else said: "I have a Junzi bamboo." Another said: "I've got a canna." One said, "I've got a star green." Yet another said: "I've got a Chinese rose." Douguan said: "I've got a sister flower." The others could not match this. Then Xiangling said: "I've got a twin orchid." Douguan was not convinced, and an argument ensued between them.

## 陶谦三让徐州

曹兵围困徐州，刘备领兵解了徐州之围，徐州太守陶谦二次让徐州与刘备，刘备哪里肯受；又求刘备兵驻小沛，保护徐州，刘备才答应下来。这年陶谦六十三岁，忽然染病，派人请刘备来徐州商议军务。陶谦请刘备入卧内说："老夫病已危笃，朝夕难保；万望明公可怜汉家城池为重，受取徐州牌印。"刘备终是推托。陶谦以手指心而死。众军举哀毕，即捧牌印交刘备。刘备固辞。次日，徐州百姓拥挤府前拜哭，关、张二人亦再三相劝，刘备才接领徐州事。

## TAO QIAN OFFERS XUZHOU THREE TIMES

This is a story from The Three Kingdoms. Cao's troops surrounded Xuzhou.
Liu Bei took his army to defeat Cao's troops and saved the city of Xuzhou.
Tao Qian, the governor of Xuzhou, offered Xuzhou to Liu Bei twice, but was
refused by him. Tao Qian then asked Liu Bei to station his army at Xiaopei
County to protect Xuzhou. Liu Bei agreed. That year Tao Qian was sixty-three
years old. One day, he was sick. He dispatched a man to invite Liu Bei to
discuss military affairs in Xuzhou. Tao Qian led Liu Bei to his room and said:
"I'm seriously ill and my life is coming to an end. Please take this poor city of
the Han court into consideration and receive the seal of Xuzhou." Liu Bei
again refused to take it. Tao Qian pointed at his heart with his finger and died.
All the soldiers and generals wailed in mourning, and handed the seal over to
Liu Bei, who made his excuses and left. The next day, the people of Xuzhou
flocked to Liu Bei's mansion, crying and kowtowing. Guan Yunchang and
Zhang Fei persuaded Liu Bei again and again. In the end Liu Bei took over the
affairs of Xuzhou.

## 吕无病

洛阳公子孙麟，娶蒋太守女儿为妻，甚是恩爱。不幸，妻子早逝，孙麟悲伤不已，离家居住山中别墅。一日阴雨，一年约十八九岁女子卷帘而入，自称吕无病，仰慕公子世家名士，愿当婢女。孙麟纳她为妾，又娶许氏为妻。许氏甚贤，对无病如姊妹。许氏生子阿坚，无病视为己出疼爱。阿坚三岁，母病故。孙麟又娶吏部

## LÜ WUBING

This is a story from Strange Tales from the Make-Do Studio. Sun Lin, the son of a high official from Luoyang, married the daughter of the governor Jiang. The couple loved each other very much. Unfortunately, the wife died early. Sun Lin was so sad that he left his home and went to live in his villa in the mountains. One rainy day, an eighteen-year-old girl entered his room. She told him that her name was Lü Wubing, and that she was willing to be his maid because she respected the fame of his family. Sun Lin took her as his concubine and married Lady Xu as his second wife. Lady Xu was very genial and prudent. She treated Lü Wubing as her own sister. Lady Xu gave a birth to a son named Ajian. Lü Wubing loved the boy very much. When

王天官女。此女其貌艳美，性情暴戾，看无病一无是处，并迁怒于丈夫，吵得全家不宁。孙麟逃避恶妇，离家远行。恶妇对阿坚非骂即打，致使阿坚有病，终日啼哭。无病抱起阿坚离家出走，寻他父亲。无病寻到孙麟，倒地死去，只见衣履不见人。孙麟才知无病是鬼，念其仁义，葬其衣履，立碑刻字："鬼妻吕无病之墓"。这是《聊斋志异》中故事。

Ajian was three, his mother died of illness. Sun Lin once again married the daughter of an official, this time of Wang from the Board of Civil Offices. The new wife was extremely pretty, but bad-tempered. She often found fault with Lü Wubing and took it out on her husband, making a lot of trouble within the family. Sun Lin left home and went on a trip to distance places to escape his evil wife. The new wife either scolded Ajian or beat him, making him ill and causing him to cry constantly. Lü Wubing took Ajian and left to look for his father. When Lü Wubing found Sun Lin, she fell down and died leaving no trace of her body, only her clothes and shoes. It was then that Sun Lin realized that she was a devil, but for the sake of her benevolence, Sun Lin buried her clothes and shoes and erected a stone tablet on which inscribed: "Tomb of a Devil Wife Lü Wubing."

## 画 皮

山西太原王生，路遇一美貌少女，勾引回家中书房私通。一天，道士在集市上看见王生说："你一身鬼气，死在临头。"王生不信，回到家里，见书房紧闭。他在窗下往里面偷看，见一青面獠牙恶

## A PAINTED HIDE

This is a story from Strange Tales of the Make-Do Studio. Wang Sheng from Taiyuan, Shanxi met a beautiful girl and brought her home to live with him. One day, a Taoist priest saw Wang Sheng in the market and said to him, "You have an evil vapour in your body and are doomed to die." Wang Sheng did not believe him. On his return, seeing the door of his study was closed, he peeped

鬼，在画一张人皮，画好后往身上一披一抖，就变成了美丽少女。
王生胆战心惊地躲进妻子房间，不敢出屋一步。一更时分，那鬼
闯进屋中，走近卧床，撕开王生胸膛，挖出王生心脏而走。这是
《聊斋志异》中一段故事，图中正是披着画皮的恶鬼。

in through the window and saw a fierce-looking devil painting a hide.
Then the devil draped the hide over its body and changed into a beautiful
girl. Wang Sheng was terrified. He hid himself in his wife's room and
dared not step outside. At the first watch, the devil broke into the room
and walked to his bedside. She then tore open Wang Sheng's chest, took
his heart out and left. The girl in this painting is the devil in hide.

**图书在版编目（CIP）数据**

颐和园长廊彩画故事／张大明编著. —北京：新世界出版社，2002.3

ISBN 7-80005-706-2

I. 颐... II. 张... III. 英语－对照读物－英、汉 IV. H319. 4

中国版本图书馆CIP数据核字（2002）第009954号

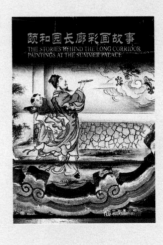

## 颐和园长廊彩画故事

名誉主编：李福瀛，段应合
主　　编：张大明
责任编辑：郭林祥
外文责编：李淑娟
摄　　影：游　牧，李维深，王兆辉，杨福生
设　　计：徐沪生
出版发行：新世界出版社
社　　址：北京百万庄路24号
邮政编码：100037
电子邮件：nwpcn@public.bta.net.cn

印　　刷：北京利丰雅高长城印刷有限公司
　　　　　2002年3月第1版 2002年3月第1次印刷
　　　　　32开／6.5印张
　　　　　02000